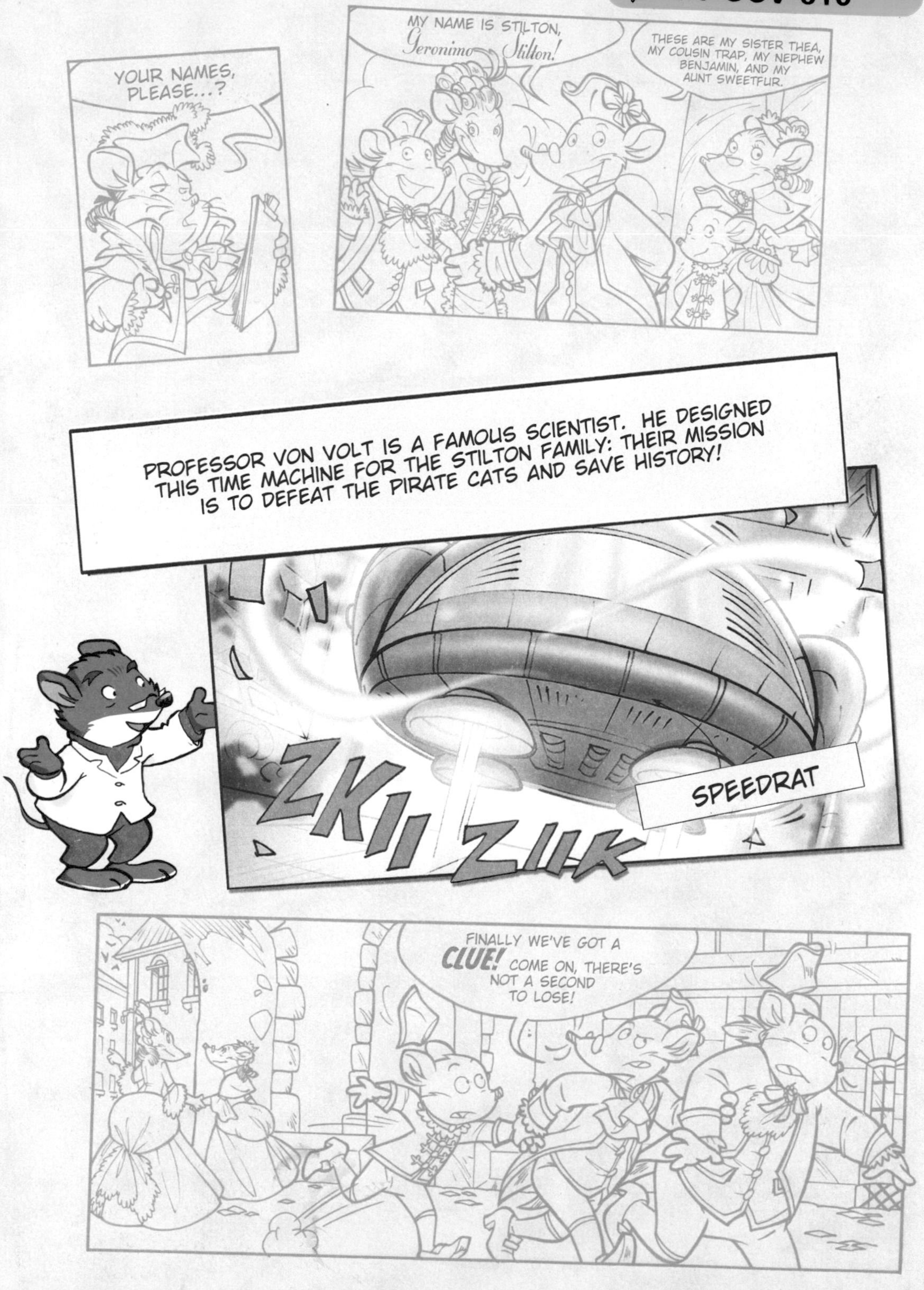
YOUR NAMES, PLEASE...?
MY NAME IS STILTON, Geronimo Stilton!
THESE ARE MY SISTER THEA, MY COUSIN TRAP, MY NEPHEW BENJAMIN, AND MY AUNT SWEETFUR.
PROFESSOR VON VOLT IS A FAMOUS SCIENTIST. HE DESIGNED THIS TIME MACHINE FOR THE STILTON FAMILY: THEIR MISSION IS TO DEFEAT THE PIRATE CATS AND SAVE HISTORY!
ZKII ZIIK
SPEEDRAT
FINALLY WE'VE GOT A CLUE! COME ON, THERE'S NOT A SECOND TO LOSE!

# Geronimo Stilton

# PLAY IT AGAIN, MOZART!

PAPERCUTZ™

# Geronimo Stilton

## PLAY IT AGAIN, MOZART!

### By Geronimo Stilton

New York

Text by Geronimo Stilton
Editorial coordination by Patrizia Puricelli
Script by Leonardi Favia
Artistic coordination by BAO Publishing
Illustrations by Federica Salfo and color by Manuela Nerolini
Based on an original idea by Elisabetta Dami

Original title:  Geronimo Stilton Suonala Ancora, Mozart!

Translation by: Nanette McGuinness

www.geronimostilton.com

Lettering and Production by Ortho
Michael Petranek – Associate Editor
Jim Salicrup
Editor-in-Chief

ISBN: 978-1-59707-276-2

Printed in China.

August 2015 by WKT Co. LTD.
3/F Phase 1 Leader Industrial Centre
188 Texaco Road, Tsuen Wan, N.T.
Hong Kong

Distributed by Macmillan.
Fourth Papercutz Printing

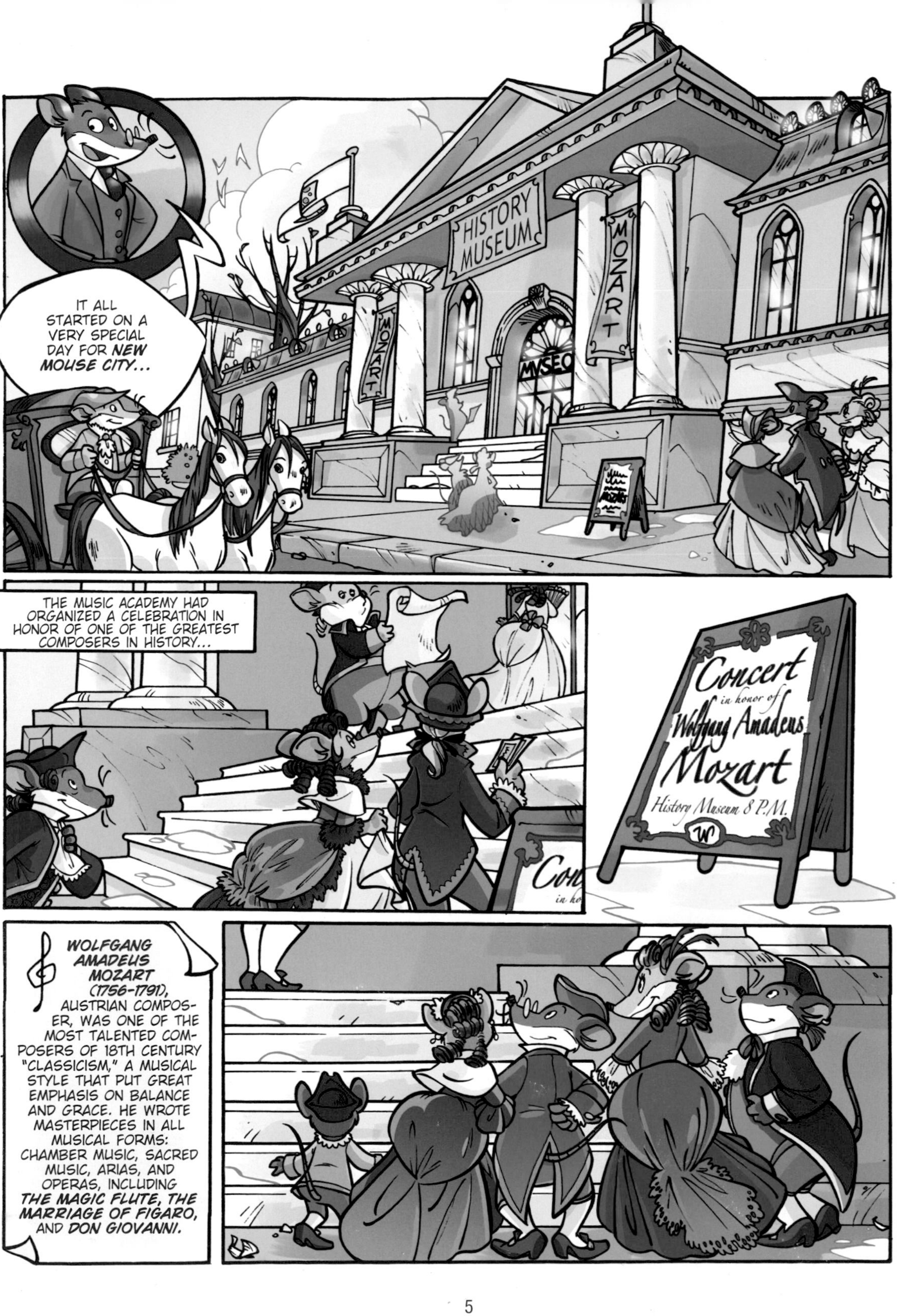
IT ALL STARTED ON A VERY SPECIAL DAY FOR NEW MOUSE CITY...
HISTORY MUSEUM
MOZART
MOZART
MVSEO
THE MUSIC ACADEMY HAD ORGANIZED A CELEBRATION IN HONOR OF ONE OF THE GREATEST COMPOSERS IN HISTORY...
Concert in honor of Wolfgang Amadeus Mozart
History Museum 8 P.M.
WOLFGANG AMADEUS MOZART (1756-1791), AUSTRIAN COMPOSER, WAS ONE OF THE MOST TALENTED COMPOSERS OF 18TH CENTURY "CLASSICISM," A MUSICAL STYLE THAT PUT GREAT EMPHASIS ON BALANCE AND GRACE. HE WROTE MASTERPIECES IN ALL MUSICAL FORMS: CHAMBER MUSIC, SACRED MUSIC, ARIAS, AND OPERAS, INCLUDING THE MAGIC FLUTE, THE MARRIAGE OF FIGARO, AND DON GIOVANNI.

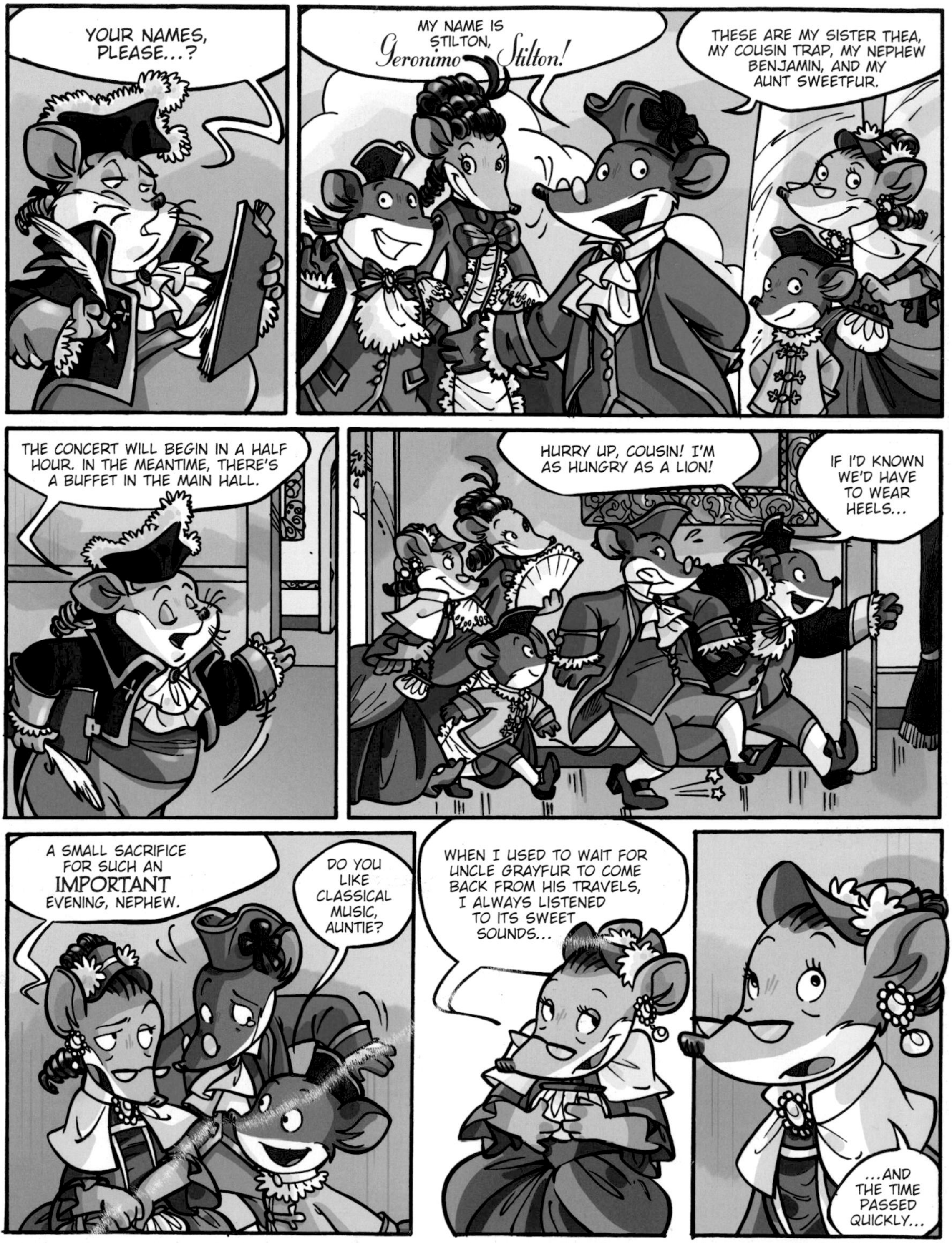
YOUR NAMES, PLEASE...?
MY NAME IS STILTON, Geronimo Stilton!
THESE ARE MY SISTER THEA, MY COUSIN TRAP, MY NEPHEW BENJAMIN, AND MY AUNT SWEETFUR.
THE CONCERT WILL BEGIN IN A HALF HOUR. IN THE MEANTIME, THERE'S A BUFFET IN THE MAIN HALL.
HURRY UP, COUSIN! I'M AS HUNGRY AS A LION!
IF I'D KNOWN WE'D HAVE TO WEAR HEELS...
A SMALL SACRIFICE FOR SUCH AN IMPORTANT EVENING, NEPHEW.
DO YOU LIKE CLASSICAL MUSIC, AUNTIE?
WHEN I USED TO WAIT FOR UNCLE GRAYFUR TO COME BACK FROM HIS TRAVELS, I ALWAYS LISTENED TO ITS SWEET SOUNDS...
...AND THE TIME PASSED QUICKLY...

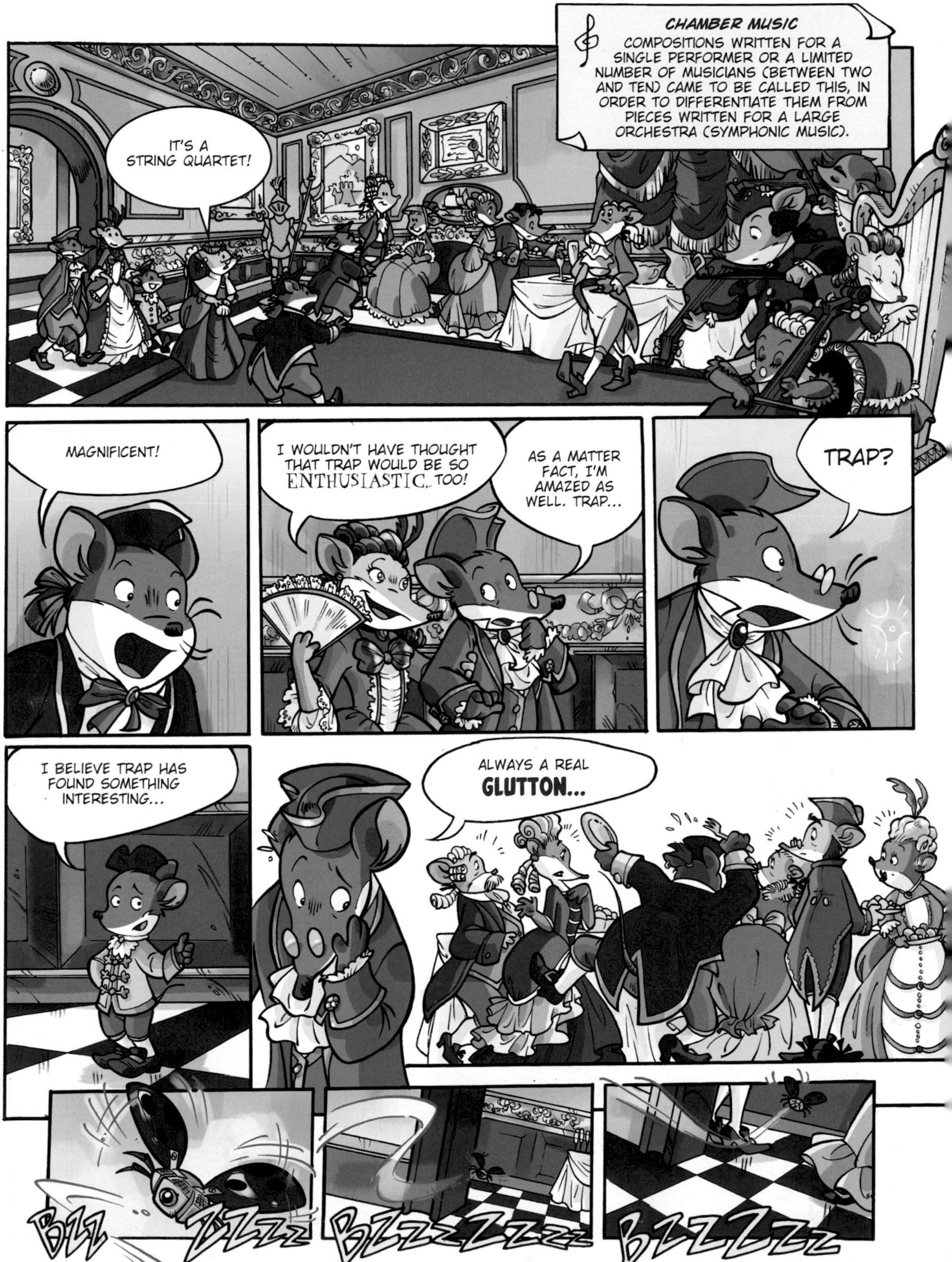
CHAMBER MUSIC
COMPOSITIONS WRITTEN FOR A SINGLE PERFORMER OR A LIMITED NUMBER OF MUSICIANS (BETWEEN TWO AND TEN) CAME TO BE CALLED THIS, IN ORDER TO DIFFERENTIATE THEM FROM PIECES WRITTEN FOR A LARGE ORCHESTRA (SYMPHONIC MUSIC).
IT'S A STRING QUARTET!
MAGNIFICENT!
I WOULDN'T HAVE THOUGHT THAT TRAP WOULD BE SO ENTHUSIASTIC... TOO!
AS A MATTER FACT, I'M AMAZED AS WELL. TRAP...
TRAP?
I BELIEVE TRAP HAS FOUND SOMETHING INTERESTING...
ALWAYS A REAL GLUTTON...
BZZ
BZZZZ
BZZZZZZZZZ
BZZZZZZZ

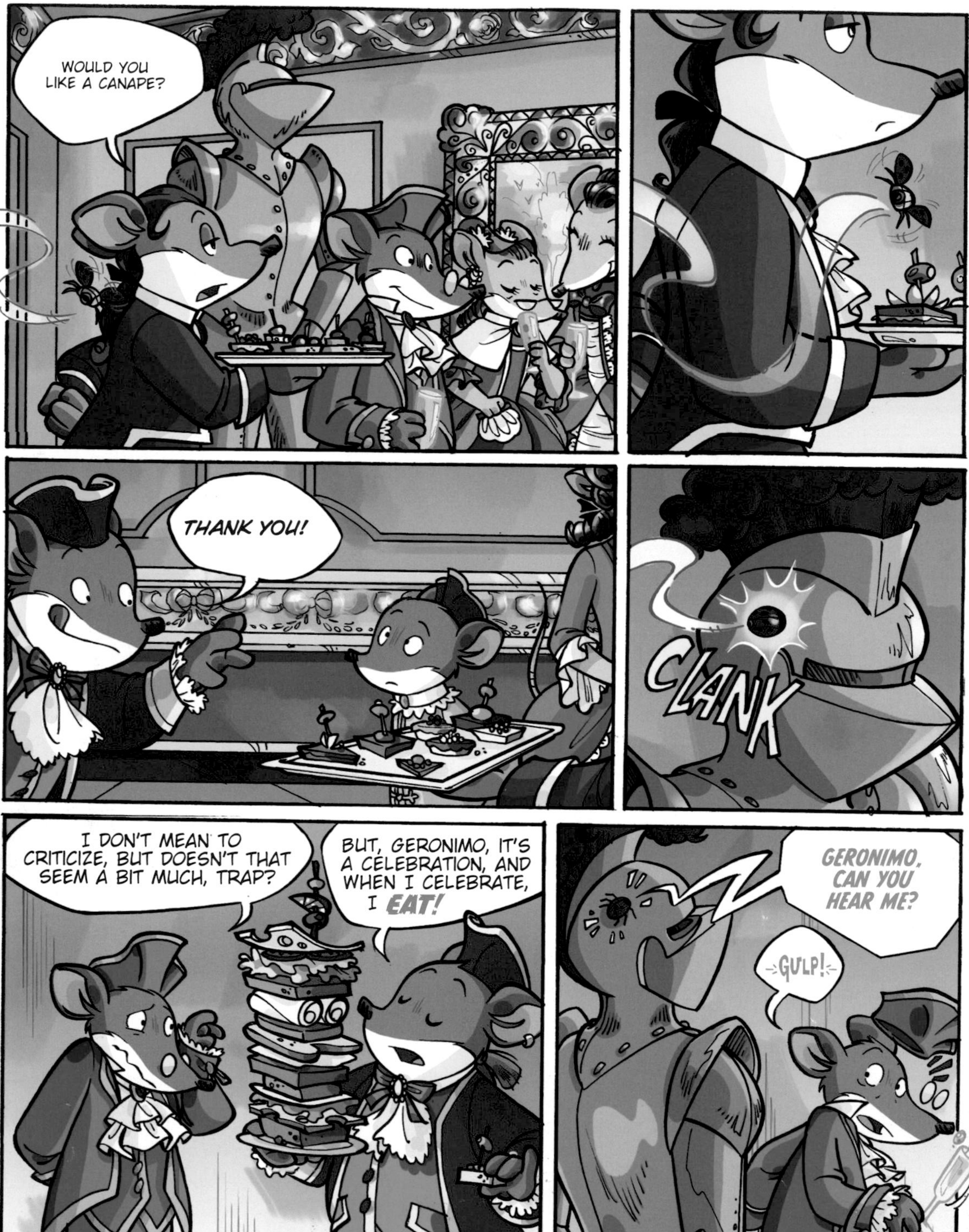
WOULD YOU LIKE A CANAPE?
THANK YOU!
CLANK
I DON'T MEAN TO CRITICIZE, BUT DOESN'T THAT SEEM A BIT MUCH, TRAP?
BUT, GERONIMO, IT'S A CELEBRATION, AND WHEN I CELEBRATE, I EAT!
GERONIMO. CAN YOU HEAR ME?
GULP!

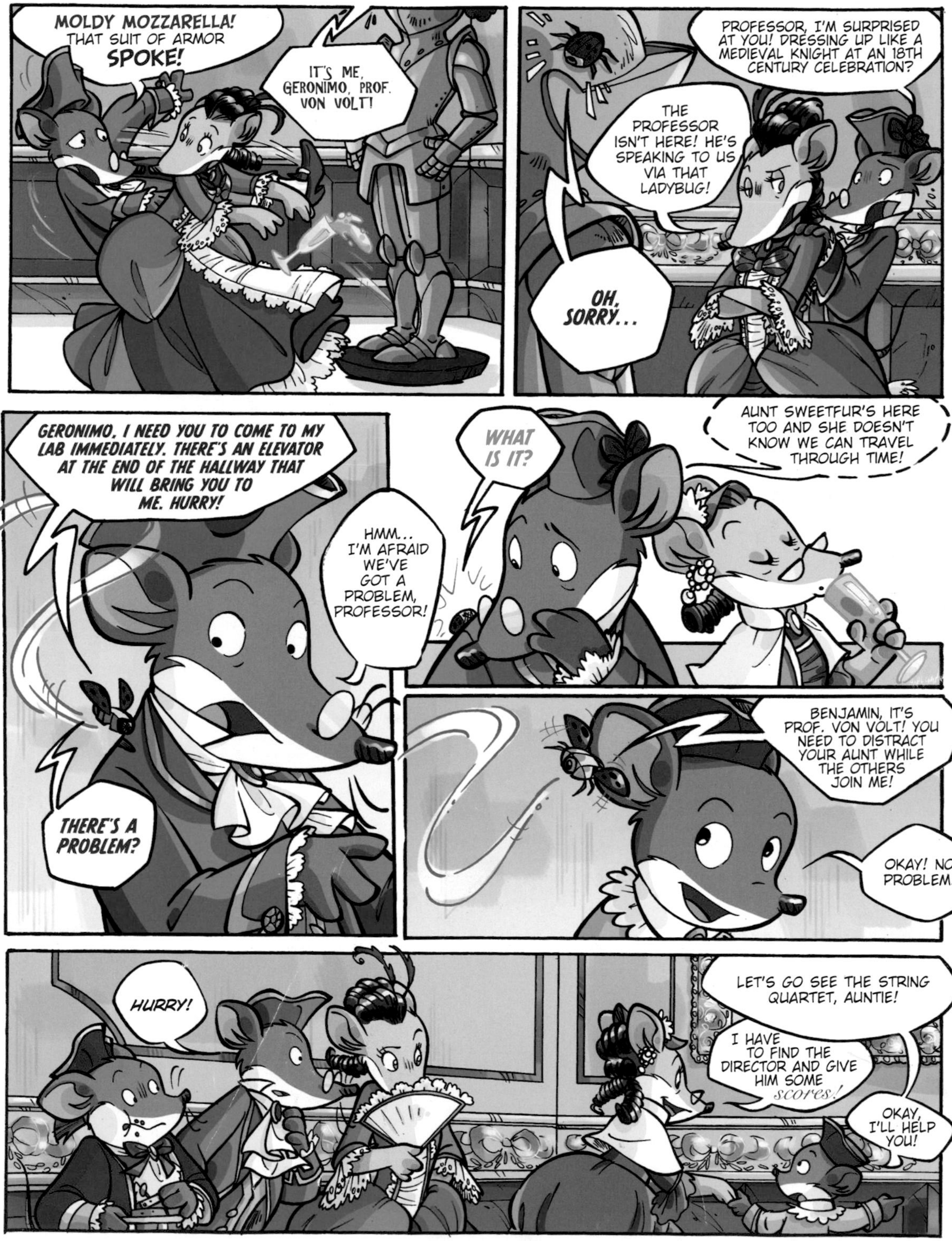
MOLDY MOZZARELLA! THAT SUIT OF ARMOR SPOKE!
IT'S ME, GERONIMO, PROF. VON VOLT!
PROFESSOR, I'M SURPRISED AT YOU! DRESSING UP LIKE A MEDIEVAL KNIGHT AT AN 18TH CENTURY CELEBRATION?
THE PROFESSOR ISN'T HERE! HE'S SPEAKING TO US VIA THAT LADYBUG!
OH, SORRY...
GERONIMO, I NEED YOU TO COME TO MY LAB IMMEDIATELY. THERE'S AN ELEVATOR AT THE END OF THE HALLWAY THAT WILL BRING YOU TO ME. HURRY!
HMM... I'M AFRAID WE'VE GOT A PROBLEM, PROFESSOR!
THERE'S A PROBLEM?
WHAT IS IT?
AUNT SWEETFUR'S HERE TOO AND SHE DOESN'T KNOW WE CAN TRAVEL THROUGH TIME!
BENJAMIN, IT'S PROF. VON VOLT! YOU NEED TO DISTRACT YOUR AUNT WHILE THE OTHERS JOIN ME!
OKAY! NO PROBLEM.
HURRY!
LET'S GO SEE THE STRING QUARTET, AUNTIE!
I HAVE TO FIND THE DIRECTOR AND GIVE HIM SOME scores!
OKAY, I'LL HELP YOU!

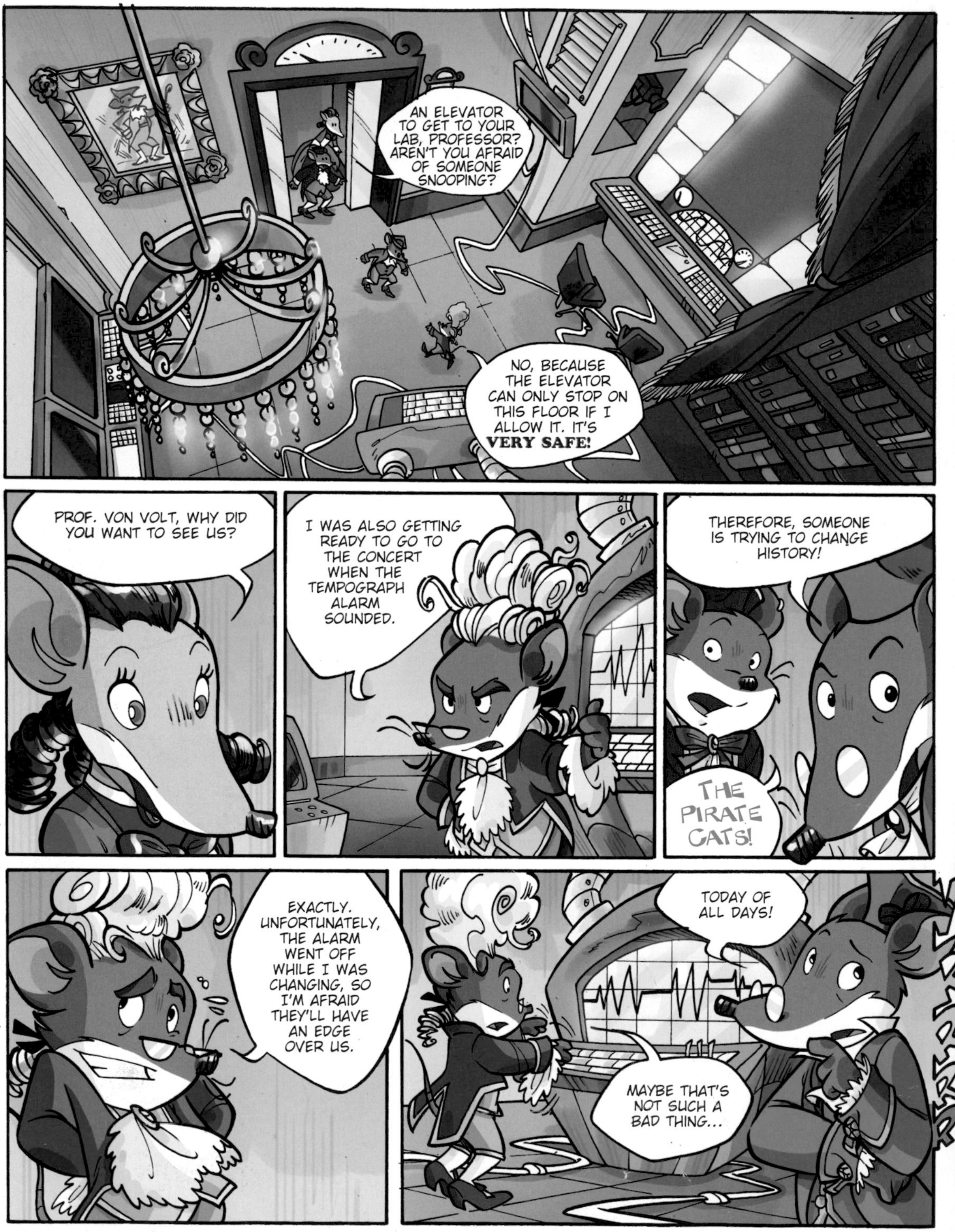
AN ELEVATOR TO GET TO YOUR LAB, PROFESSOR? AREN'T YOU AFRAID OF SOMEONE SNOOPING?
NO, BECAUSE THE ELEVATOR CAN ONLY STOP ON THIS FLOOR IF I ALLOW IT. IT'S VERY SAFE!
PROF. VON VOLT, WHY DID YOU WANT TO SEE US?
I WAS ALSO GETTING READY TO GO TO THE CONCERT WHEN THE TEMPOGRAPH ALARM SOUNDED.
THEREFORE, SOMEONE IS TRYING TO CHANGE HISTORY!
THE PIRATE CATS!
EXACTLY. UNFORTUNATELY, THE ALARM WENT OFF WHILE I WAS CHANGING, SO I'M AFRAID THEY'LL HAVE AN EDGE OVER US.
TODAY OF ALL DAYS!
MAYBE THAT'S NOT SUCH A BAD THING...

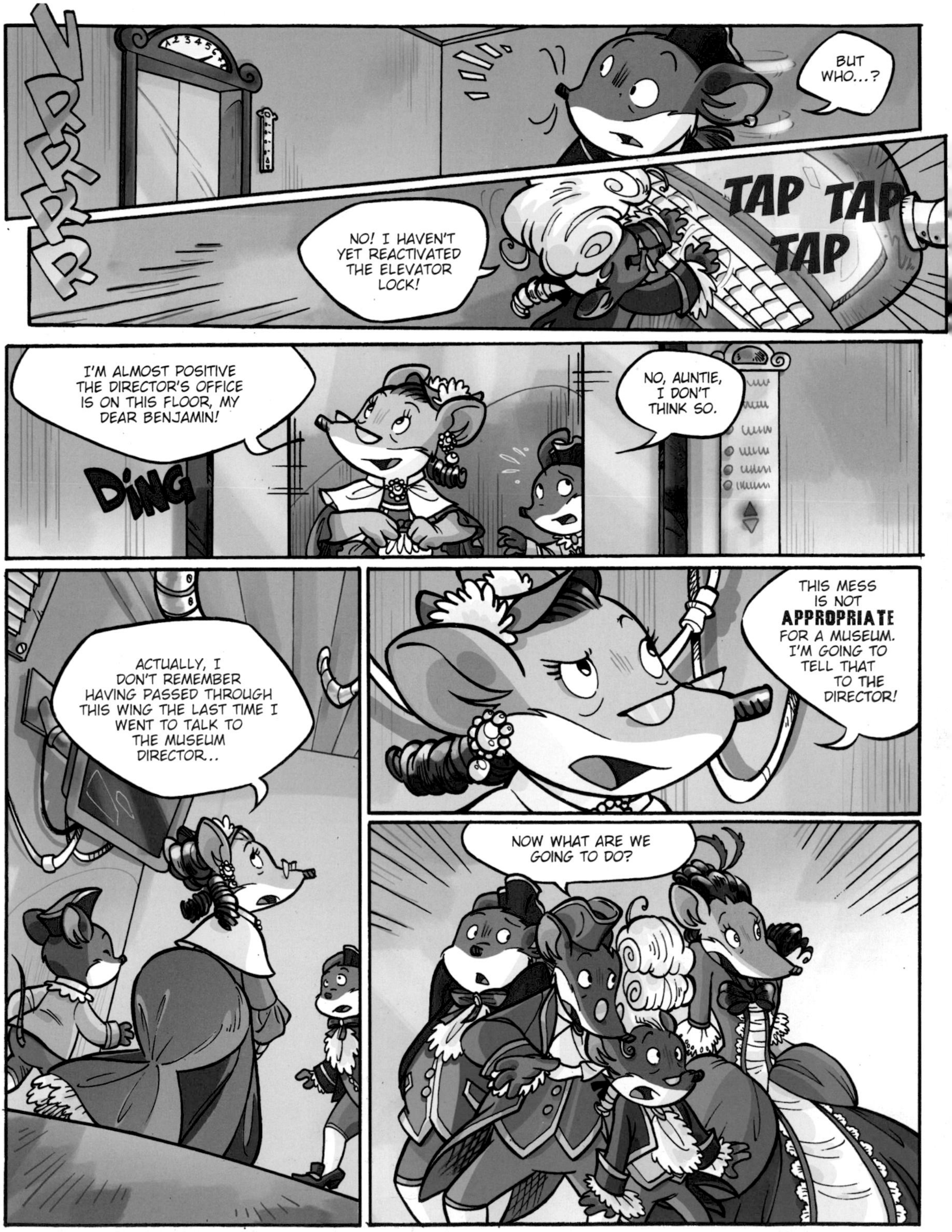
VRRRRR
BUT WHO...?
NO! I HAVEN'T YET REACTIVATED THE ELEVATOR LOCK!
TAP TAP TAP
I'M ALMOST POSITIVE THE DIRECTOR'S OFFICE IS ON THIS FLOOR, MY DEAR BENJAMIN!
DING
NO, AUNTIE, I DON'T THINK SO.
ACTUALLY, I DON'T REMEMBER HAVING PASSED THROUGH THIS WING THE LAST TIME I WENT TO TALK TO THE MUSEUM DIRECTOR...
THIS MESS IS NOT APPROPRIATE FOR A MUSEUM. I'M GOING TO TELL THAT TO THE DIRECTOR!
NOW WHAT ARE WE GOING TO DO?

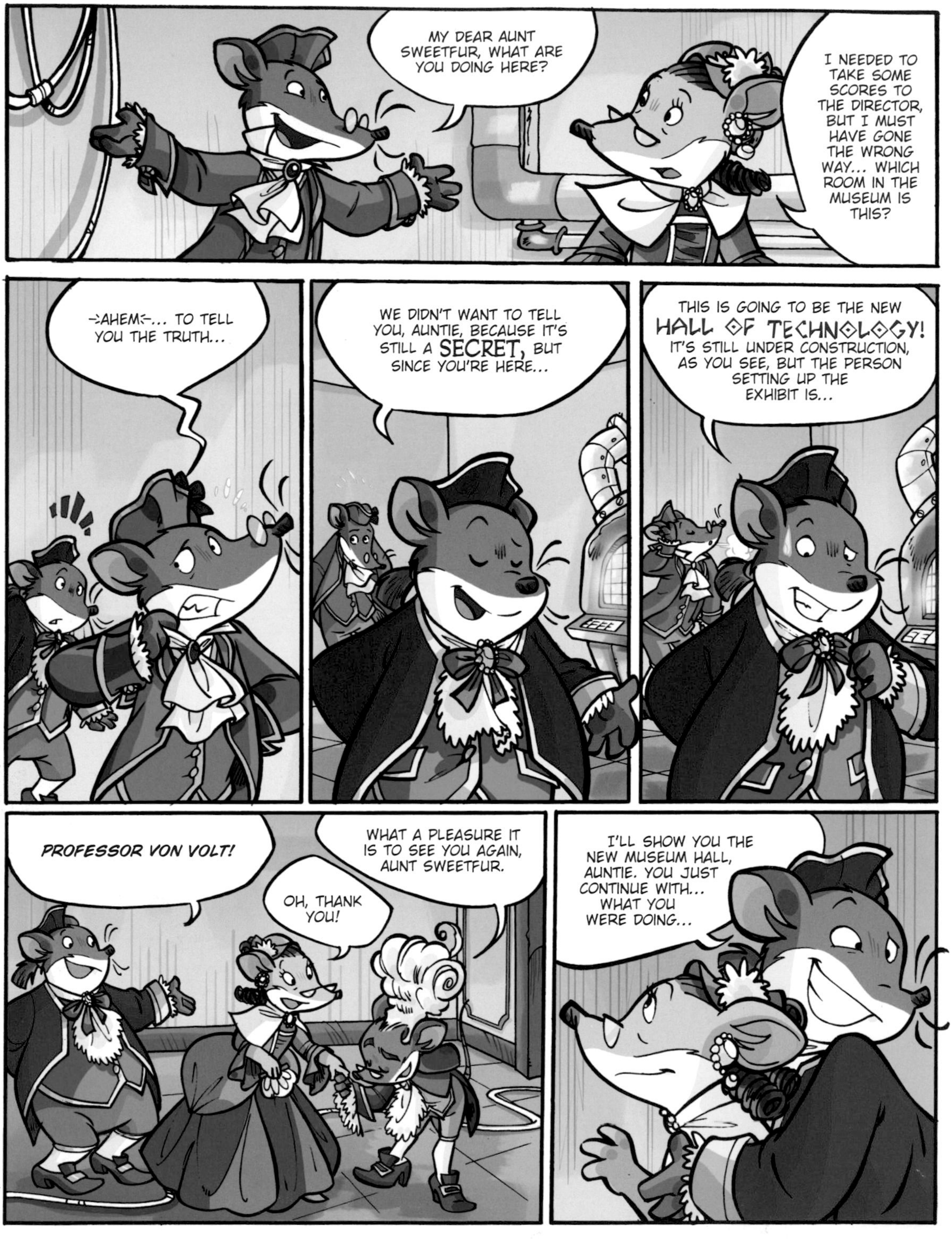

MY DEAR AUNT SWEETFUR, WHAT ARE YOU DOING HERE?
I NEEDED TO TAKE SOME SCORES TO THE DIRECTOR, BUT I MUST HAVE GONE THE WRONG WAY... WHICH ROOM IN THE MUSEUM IS THIS?
AHEM... TO TELL YOU THE TRUTH...
WE DIDN'T WANT TO TELL YOU, AUNTIE, BECAUSE IT'S STILL A SECRET, BUT SINCE YOU'RE HERE...
THIS IS GOING TO BE THE NEW HALL OF TECHNOLOGY! IT'S STILL UNDER CONSTRUCTION, AS YOU SEE, BUT THE PERSON SETTING UP THE EXHIBIT IS...
PROFESSOR VON VOLT!
WHAT A PLEASURE IT IS TO SEE YOU AGAIN, AUNT SWEETFUR.
OH, THANK YOU!
I'LL SHOW YOU THE NEW MUSEUM HALL, AUNTIE. YOU JUST CONTINUE WITH... WHAT YOU WERE DOING...

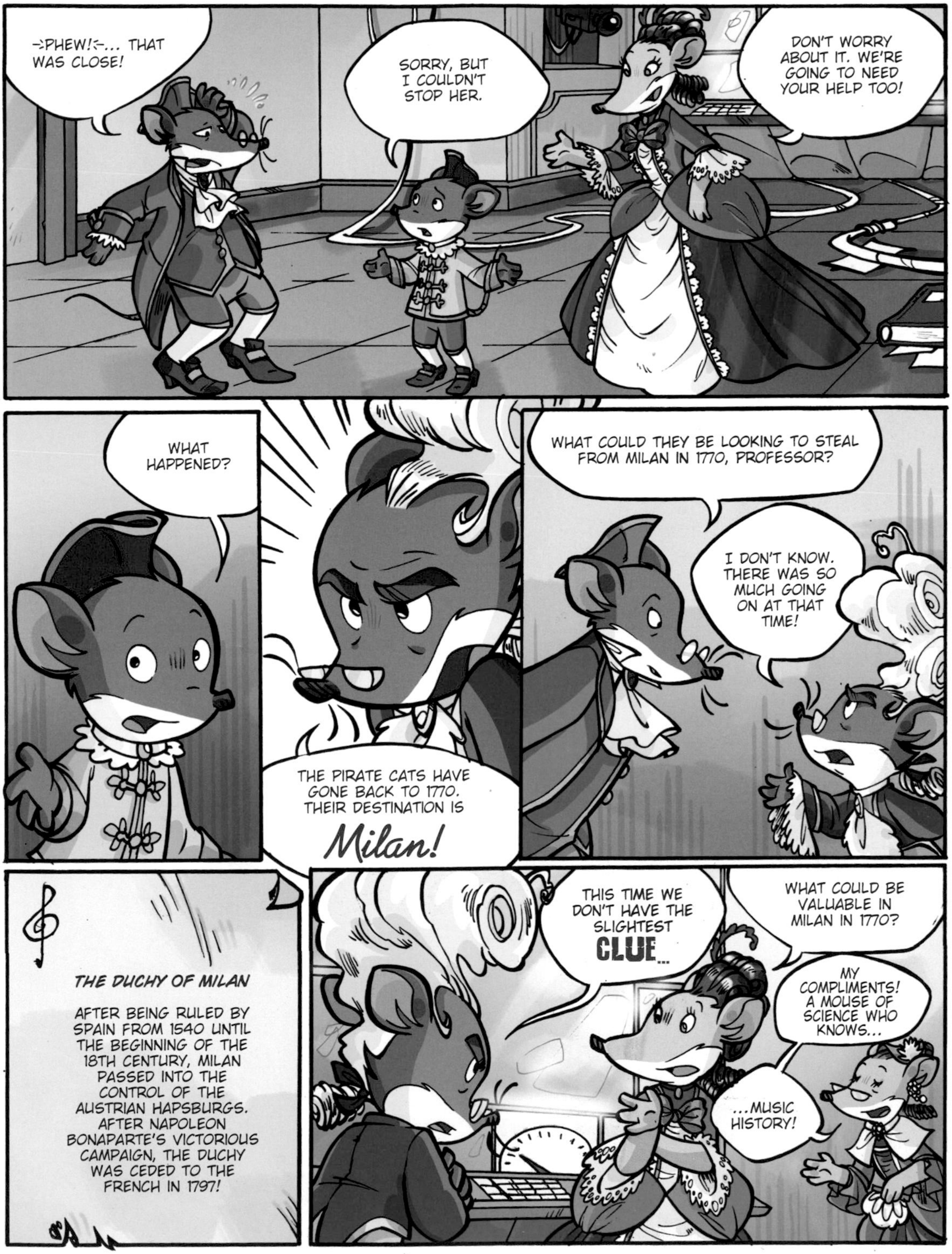

→PHEW!←... THAT WAS CLOSE!
SORRY, BUT I COULDN'T STOP HER.
DON'T WORRY ABOUT IT. WE'RE GOING TO NEED YOUR HELP TOO!
WHAT HAPPENED?
THE PIRATE CATS HAVE GONE BACK TO 1770. THEIR DESTINATION IS
Milan!
WHAT COULD THEY BE LOOKING TO STEAL FROM MILAN IN 1770, PROFESSOR?
I DON'T KNOW. THERE WAS SO MUCH GOING ON AT THAT TIME!
THE DUCHY OF MILAN
AFTER BEING RULED BY SPAIN FROM 1540 UNTIL THE BEGINNING OF THE 18TH CENTURY, MILAN PASSED INTO THE CONTROL OF THE AUSTRIAN HAPSBURGS. AFTER NAPOLEON BONAPARTE'S VICTORIOUS CAMPAIGN, THE DUCHY WAS CEDED TO THE FRENCH IN 1797!
THIS TIME WE DON'T HAVE THE SLIGHTEST CLUE...
WHAT COULD BE VALUABLE IN MILAN IN 1770?
MY COMPLIMENTS! A MOUSE OF SCIENCE WHO KNOWS...
...MUSIC HISTORY!

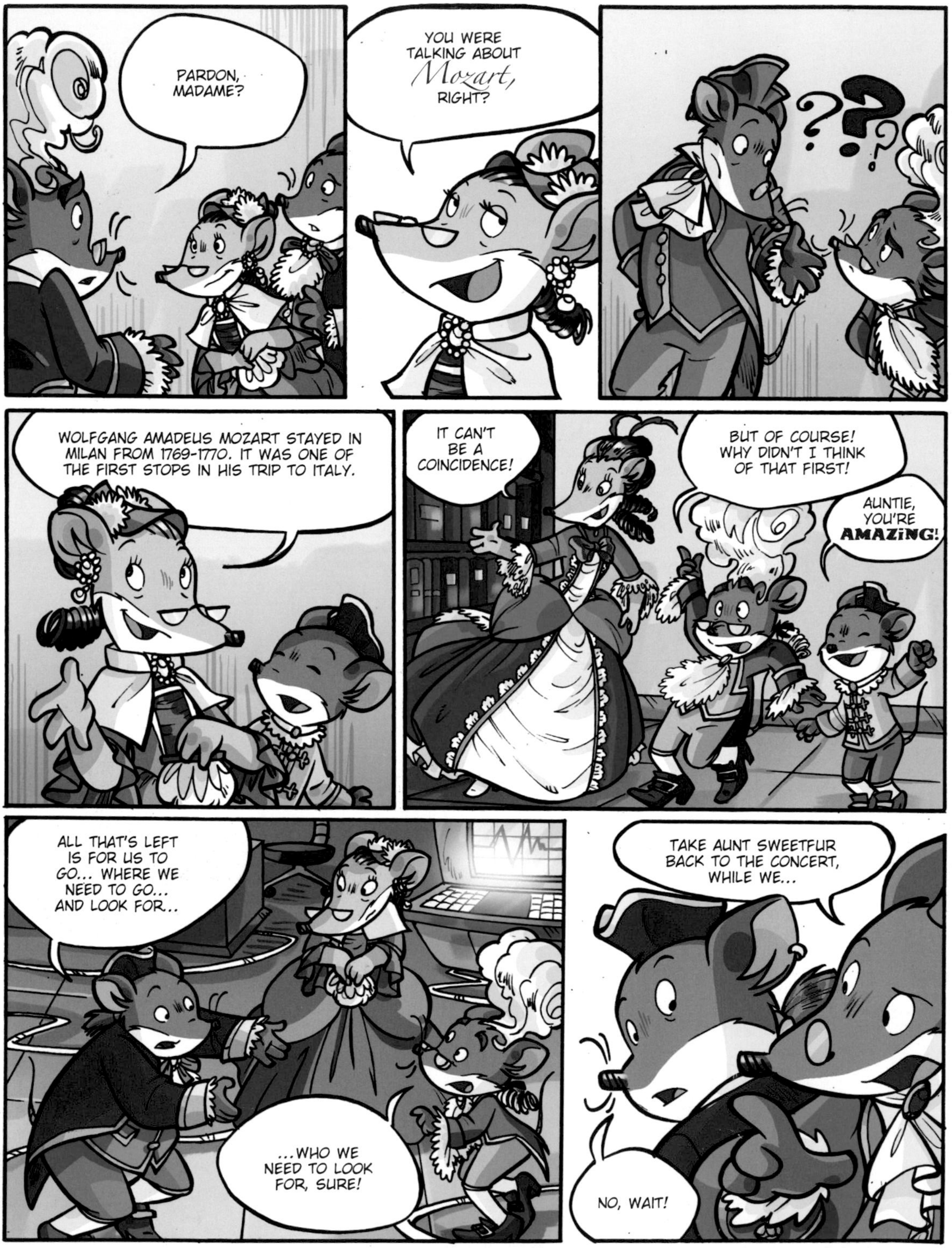
PARDON, MADAME?
YOU WERE TALKING ABOUT Mozart, RIGHT?
WOLFGANG AMADEUS MOZART STAYED IN MILAN FROM 1769-1770. IT WAS ONE OF THE FIRST STOPS IN HIS TRIP TO ITALY.
IT CAN'T BE A COINCIDENCE!
BUT OF COURSE! WHY DIDN'T I THINK OF THAT FIRST!
AUNTIE, YOU'RE AMAZING!
ALL THAT'S LEFT IS FOR US TO GO... WHERE WE NEED TO GO... AND LOOK FOR...
...WHO WE NEED TO LOOK FOR, SURE!
TAKE AUNT SWEETFUR BACK TO THE CONCERT, WHILE WE...
NO, WAIT!

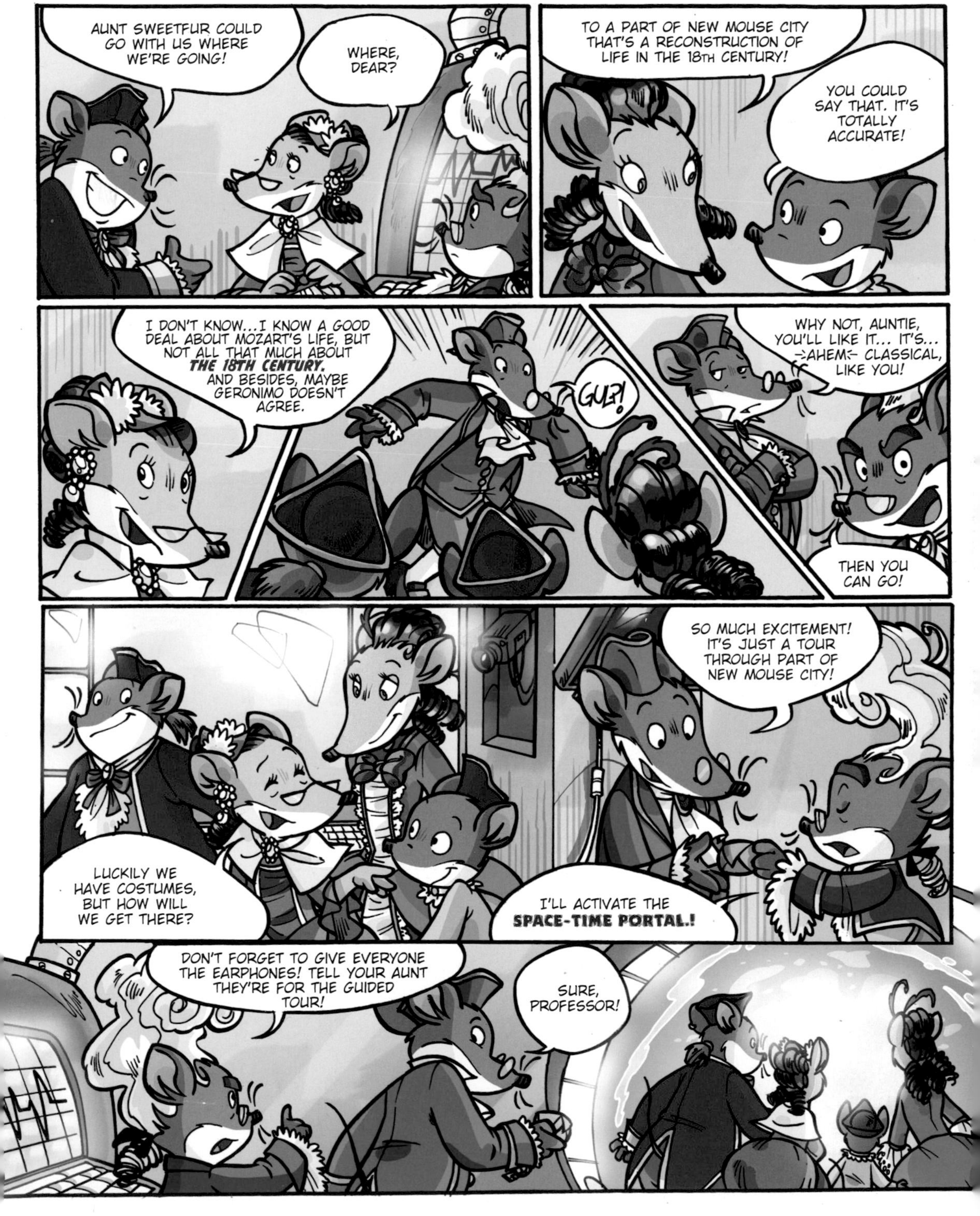
AUNT SWEETFUR COULD GO WITH US WHERE WE'RE GOING!
WHERE, DEAR?
TO A PART OF NEW MOUSE CITY THAT'S A RECONSTRUCTION OF LIFE IN THE 18TH CENTURY!
YOU COULD SAY THAT. IT'S TOTALLY ACCURATE!
I DON'T KNOW...I KNOW A GOOD DEAL ABOUT MOZART'S LIFE, BUT NOT ALL THAT MUCH ABOUT THE 18TH CENTURY. AND BESIDES, MAYBE GERONIMO DOESN'T AGREE.
GULP!
WHY NOT, AUNTIE, YOU'LL LIKE IT... IT'S... AHEM CLASSICAL, LIKE YOU!
THEN YOU CAN GO!
LUCKILY WE HAVE COSTUMES, BUT HOW WILL WE GET THERE?
SO MUCH EXCITEMENT! IT'S JUST A TOUR THROUGH PART OF NEW MOUSE CITY!
I'LL ACTIVATE THE SPACE-TIME PORTAL!
DON'T FORGET TO GIVE EVERYONE THE EARPHONES! TELL YOUR AUNT THEY'RE FOR THE GUIDED TOUR!
SURE, PROFESSOR!

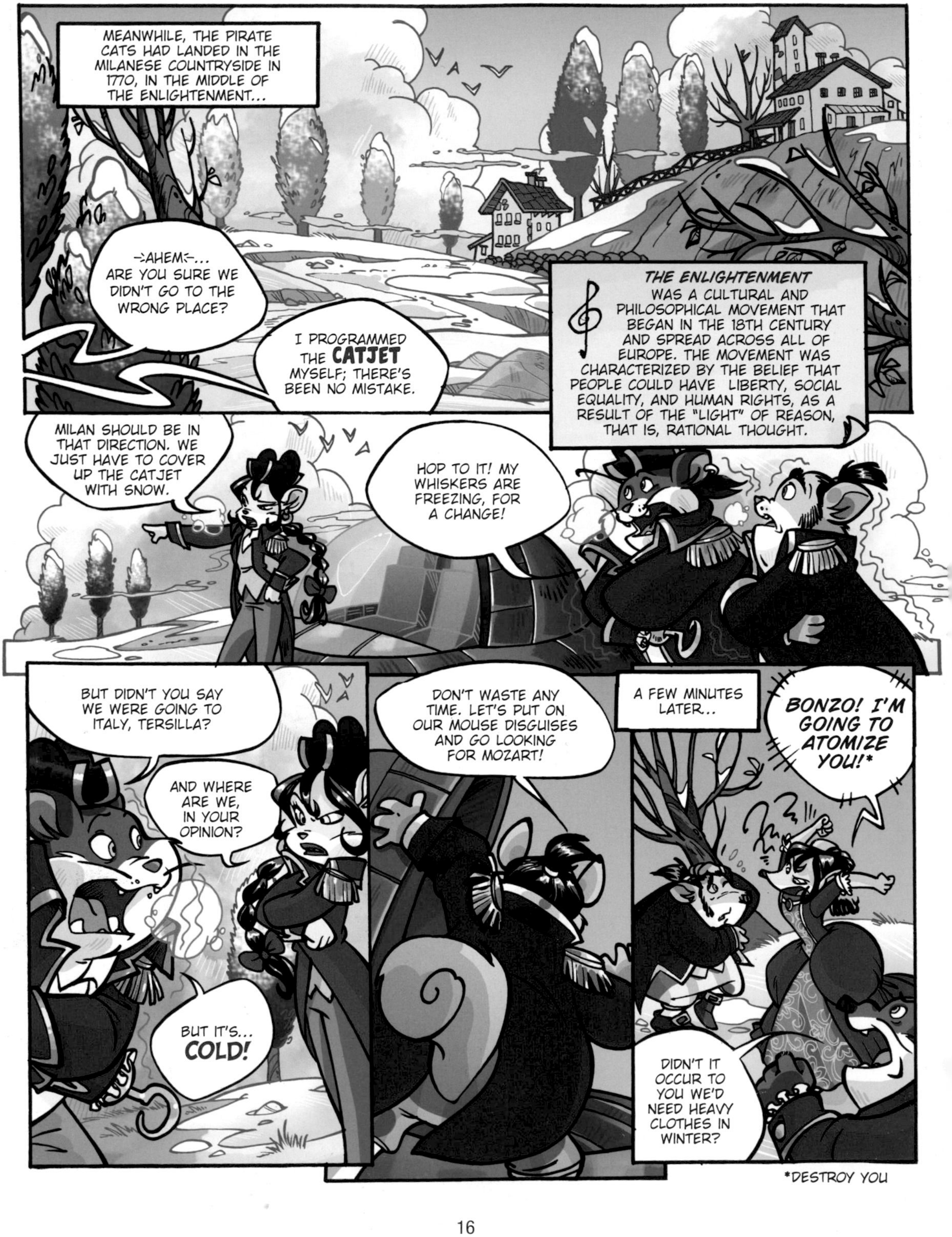
MEANWHILE, THE PIRATE CATS HAD LANDED IN THE MILANESE COUNTRYSIDE IN 1770, IN THE MIDDLE OF THE ENLIGHTENMENT...
-AHEM-... ARE YOU SURE WE DIDN'T GO TO THE WRONG PLACE?
I PROGRAMMED THE CATJET MYSELF; THERE'S BEEN NO MISTAKE.
THE ENLIGHTENMENT WAS A CULTURAL AND PHILOSOPHICAL MOVEMENT THAT BEGAN IN THE 18TH CENTURY AND SPREAD ACROSS ALL OF EUROPE. THE MOVEMENT WAS CHARACTERIZED BY THE BELIEF THAT PEOPLE COULD HAVE LIBERTY, SOCIAL EQUALITY, AND HUMAN RIGHTS, AS A RESULT OF THE "LIGHT" OF REASON, THAT IS, RATIONAL THOUGHT.
MILAN SHOULD BE IN THAT DIRECTION. WE JUST HAVE TO COVER UP THE CATJET WITH SNOW.
HOP TO IT! MY WHISKERS ARE FREEZING, FOR A CHANGE!
BUT DIDN'T YOU SAY WE WERE GOING TO ITALY, TERSILLA?
AND WHERE ARE WE, IN YOUR OPINION?
BUT IT'S... COLD!
DON'T WASTE ANY TIME. LET'S PUT ON OUR MOUSE DISGUISES AND GO LOOKING FOR MOZART!
A FEW MINUTES LATER...
BONZO! I'M GOING TO ATOMIZE YOU!*
DIDN'T IT OCCUR TO YOU WE'D NEED HEAVY CLOTHES IN WINTER?

*DESTROY YOU

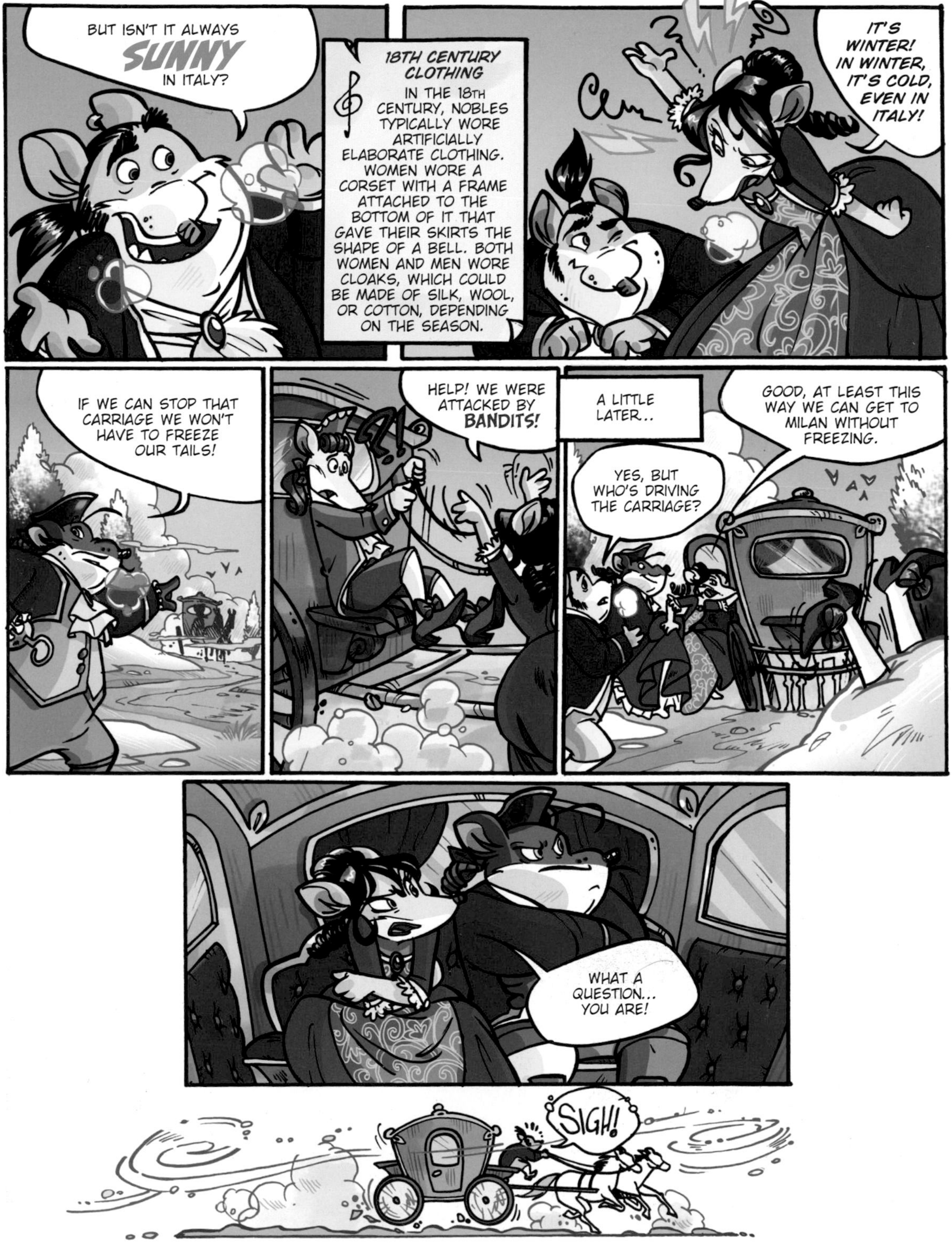

BUT ISN'T IT ALWAYS SUNNY IN ITALY?
18TH CENTURY CLOTHING
IN THE 18TH CENTURY, NOBLES TYPICALLY WORE ARTIFICIALLY ELABORATE CLOTHING. WOMEN WORE A CORSET WITH A FRAME ATTACHED TO THE BOTTOM OF IT THAT GAVE THEIR SKIRTS THE SHAPE OF A BELL. BOTH WOMEN AND MEN WORE CLOAKS, WHICH COULD BE MADE OF SILK, WOOL, OR COTTON, DEPENDING ON THE SEASON.
IT'S WINTER! IN WINTER, IT'S COLD, EVEN IN ITALY!
IF WE CAN STOP THAT CARRIAGE WE WON'T HAVE TO FREEZE OUR TAILS!
HELP! WE WERE ATTACKED BY BANDITS!
A LITTLE LATER...
GOOD, AT LEAST THIS WAY WE CAN GET TO MILAN WITHOUT FREEZING.
YES, BUT WHO'S DRIVING THE CARRIAGE?
WHAT A QUESTION... YOU ARE!
SIGH!

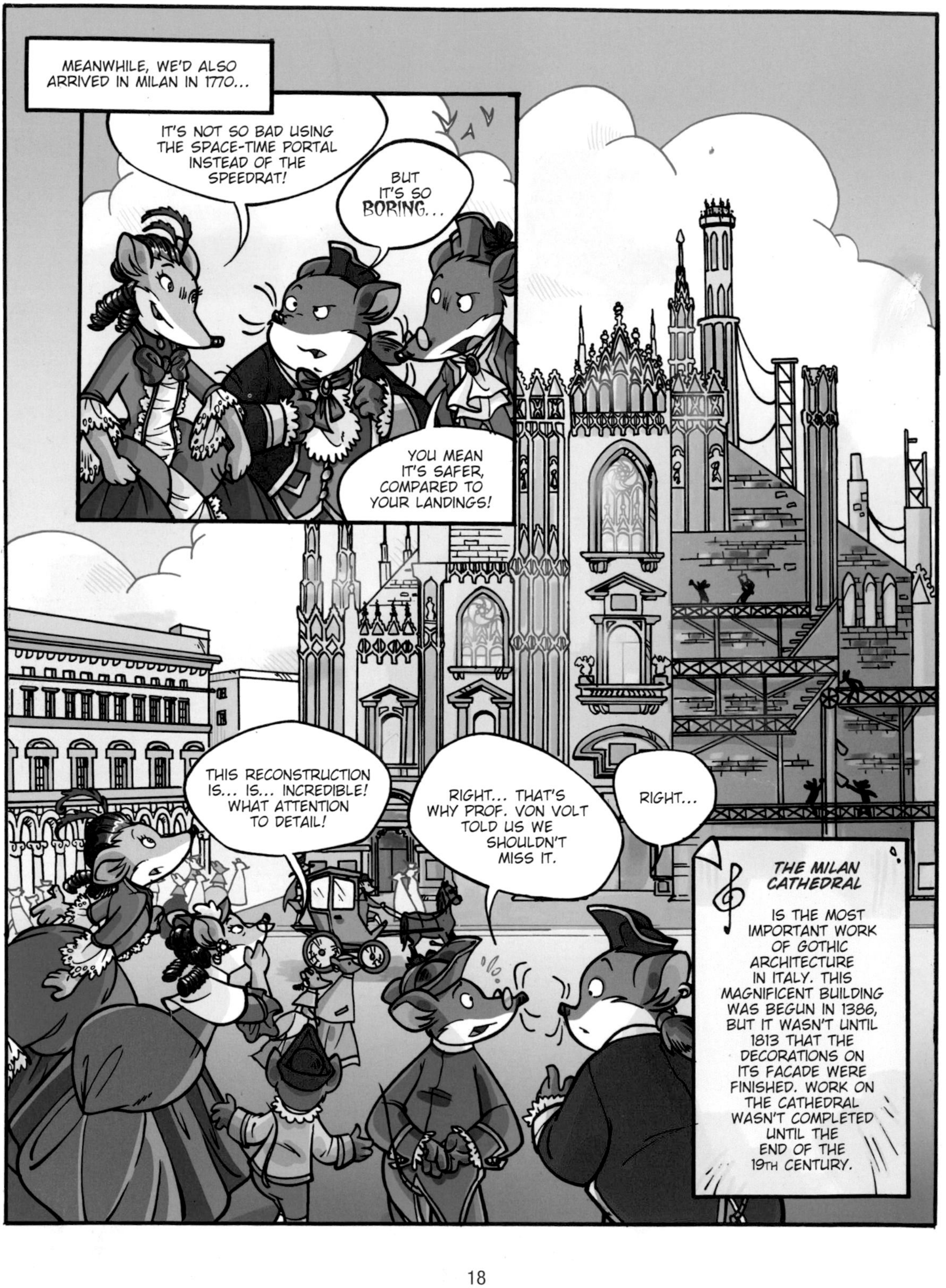
MEANWHILE, WE'D ALSO ARRIVED IN MILAN IN 1770...
IT'S NOT SO BAD USING THE SPACE-TIME PORTAL INSTEAD OF THE SPEEDRAT!
BUT IT'S SO BORING...
YOU MEAN IT'S SAFER, COMPARED TO YOUR LANDINGS!
THIS RECONSTRUCTION IS... IS... INCREDIBLE! WHAT ATTENTION TO DETAIL!
RIGHT... THAT'S WHY PROF. VON VOLT TOLD US WE SHOULDN'T MISS IT.
RIGHT...
THE MILAN CATHEDRAL
IS THE MOST IMPORTANT WORK OF GOTHIC ARCHITECTURE IN ITALY. THIS MAGNIFICENT BUILDING WAS BEGUN IN 1386, BUT IT WASN'T UNTIL 1813 THAT THE DECORATIONS ON ITS FACADE WERE FINISHED. WORK ON THE CATHEDRAL WASN'T COMPLETED UNTIL THE END OF THE 19TH CENTURY.

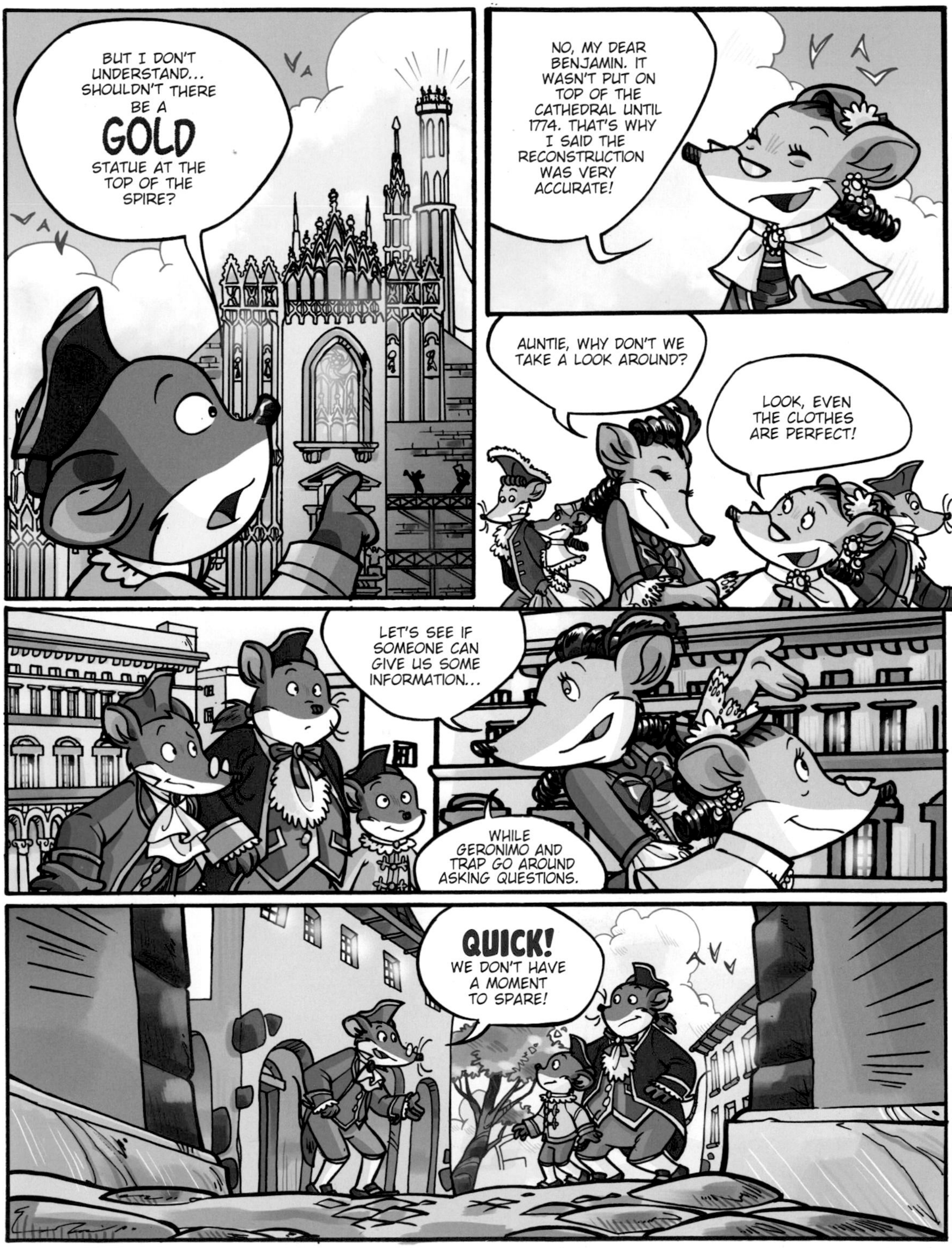
BUT I DON'T UNDERSTAND... SHOULDN'T THERE BE A GOLD STATUE AT THE TOP OF THE SPIRE?
NO, MY DEAR BENJAMIN. IT WASN'T PUT ON TOP OF THE CATHEDRAL UNTIL 1774. THAT'S WHY I SAID THE RECONSTRUCTION WAS VERY ACCURATE!
AUNTIE, WHY DON'T WE TAKE A LOOK AROUND?
LOOK, EVEN THE CLOTHES ARE PERFECT!
LET'S SEE IF SOMEONE CAN GIVE US SOME INFORMATION...
WHILE GERONIMO AND TRAP GO AROUND ASKING QUESTIONS.
QUICK! WE DON'T HAVE A MOMENT TO SPARE!

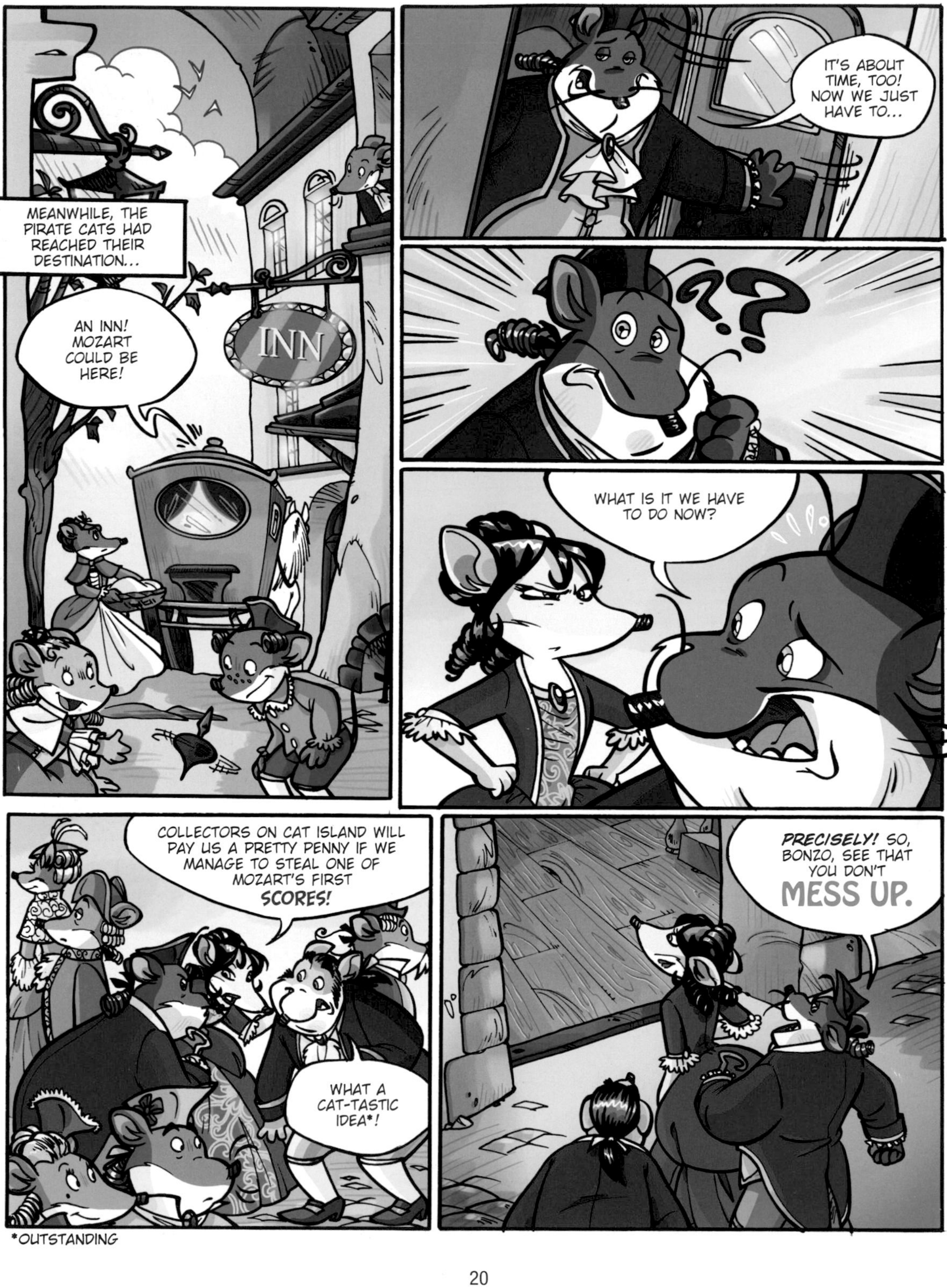
MEANWHILE, THE PIRATE CATS HAD REACHED THEIR DESTINATION...
AN INN! MOZART COULD BE HERE!
INN
IT'S ABOUT TIME, TOO! NOW WE JUST HAVE TO...
?? ?
WHAT IS IT WE HAVE TO DO NOW?
COLLECTORS ON CAT ISLAND WILL PAY US A PRETTY PENNY IF WE MANAGE TO STEAL ONE OF MOZART'S FIRST **SCORES!**
WHAT A CAT-TASTIC IDEA*!
***PRECISELY!*** SO, BONZO, SEE THAT YOU DON'T **MESS UP.**

*OUTSTANDING

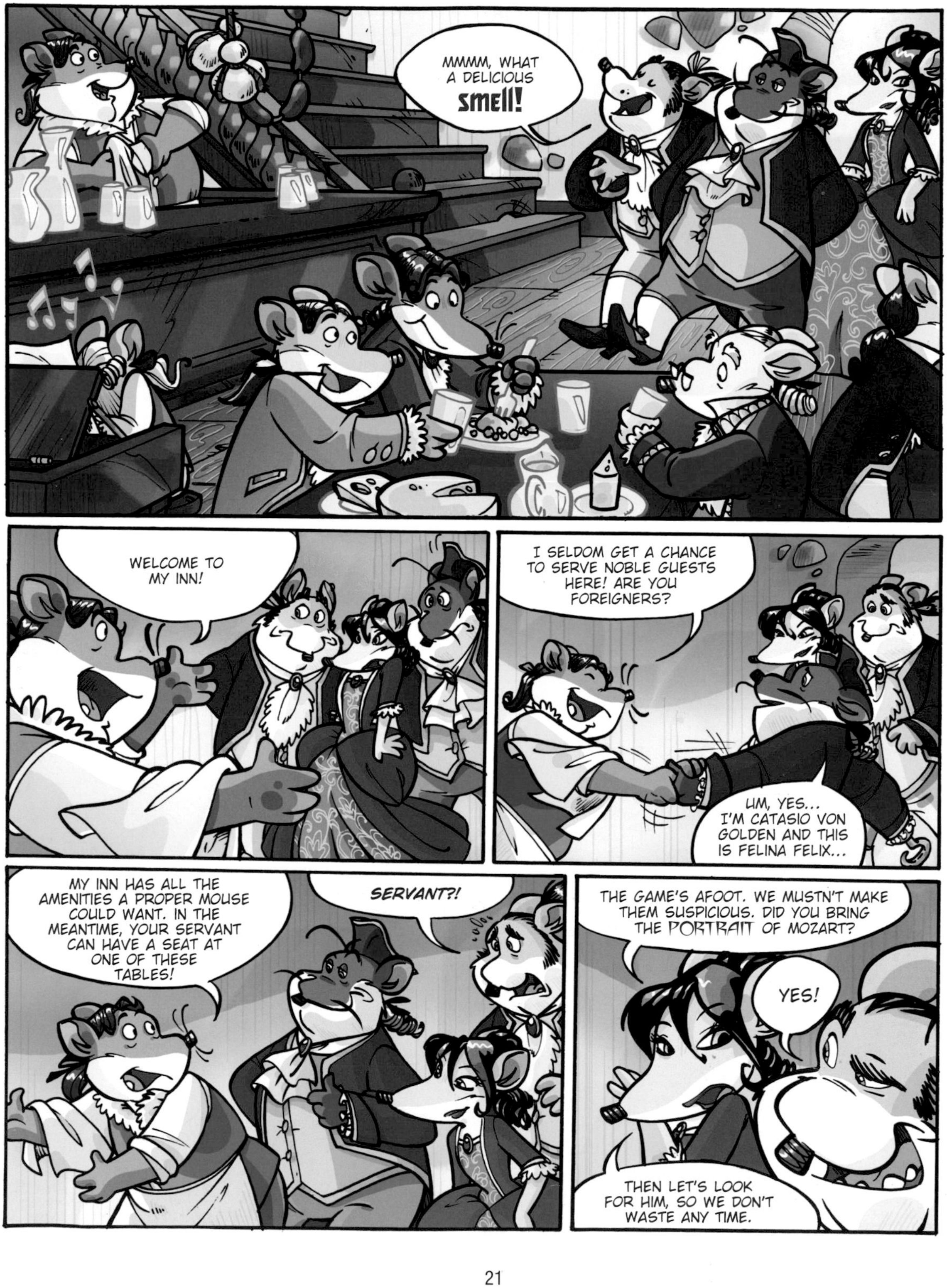
MMMM, WHAT A DELICIOUS SMELL!
WELCOME TO MY INN!
I SELDOM GET A CHANCE TO SERVE NOBLE GUESTS HERE! ARE YOU FOREIGNERS?
UM, YES... I'M CATASIO VON GOLDEN AND THIS IS FELINA FELIX...
MY INN HAS ALL THE AMENITIES A PROPER MOUSE COULD WANT. IN THE MEANTIME, YOUR SERVANT CAN HAVE A SEAT AT ONE OF THESE TABLES!
SERVANT?!
THE GAME'S AFOOT. WE MUSTN'T MAKE THEM SUSPICIOUS. DID YOU BRING THE PORTRAIT OF MOZART?
YES!
THEN LET'S LOOK FOR HIM, SO WE DON'T WASTE ANY TIME.

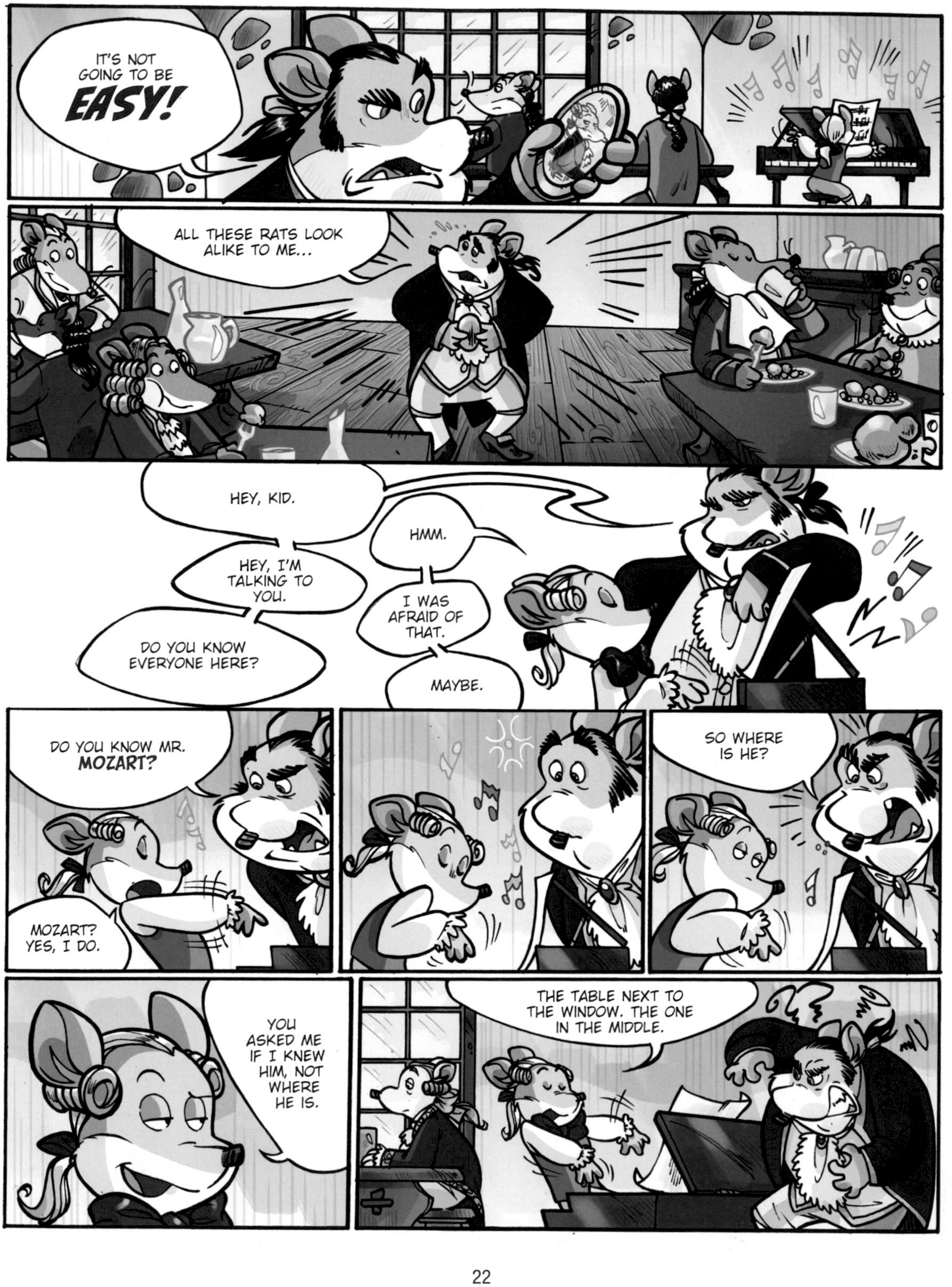
IT'S NOT GOING TO BE EASY!
ALL THESE RATS LOOK ALIKE TO ME...
HEY, KID.
HEY, I'M TALKING TO YOU.
DO YOU KNOW EVERYONE HERE?
HMM.
I WAS AFRAID OF THAT.
MAYBE.
DO YOU KNOW MR. MOZART?
MOZART? YES, I DO.
SO WHERE IS HE?
YOU ASKED ME IF I KNEW HIM, NOT WHERE HE IS.
THE TABLE NEXT TO THE WINDOW. THE ONE IN THE MIDDLE.

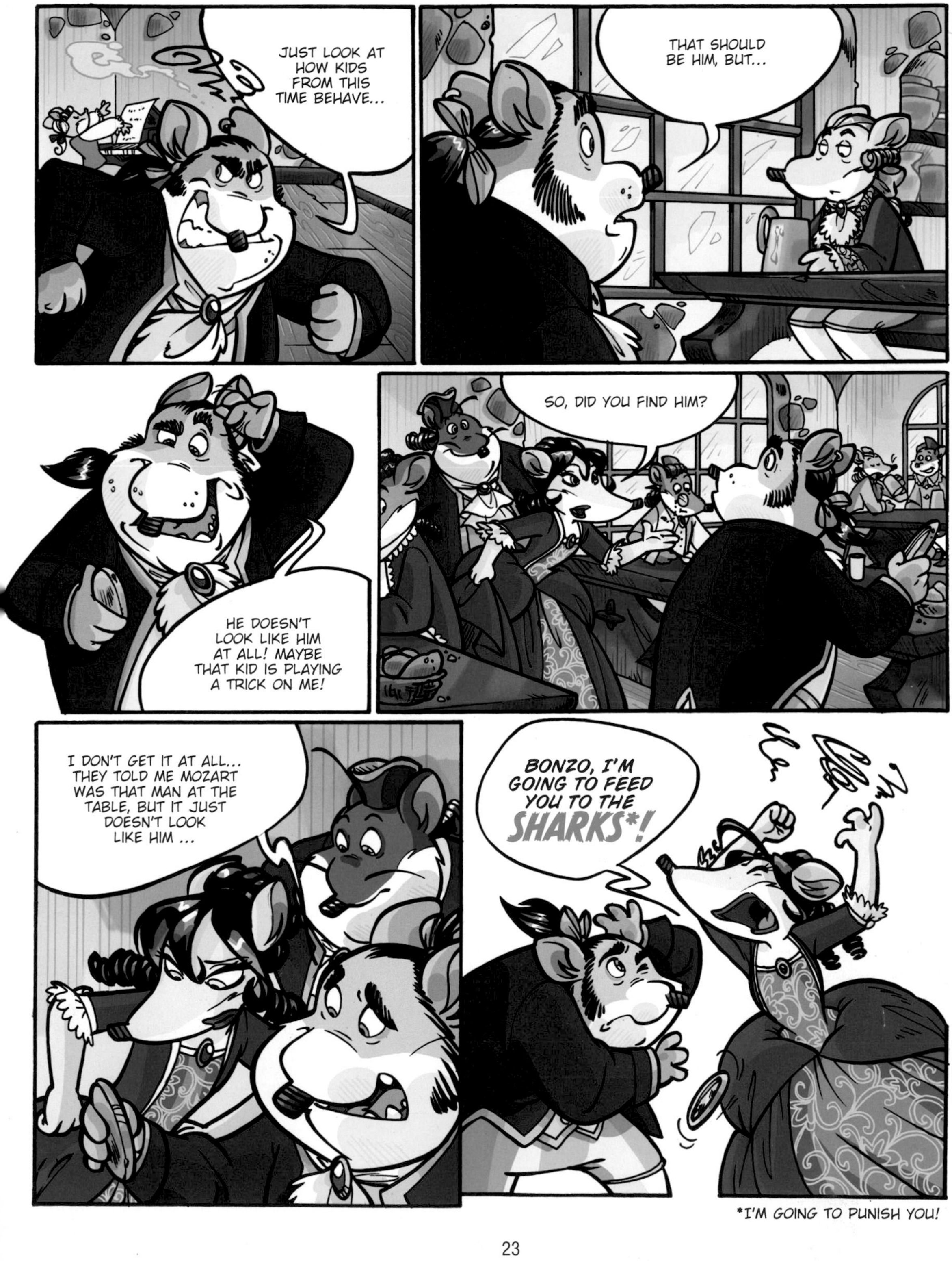
JUST LOOK AT HOW KIDS FROM THIS TIME BEHAVE...
THAT SHOULD BE HIM, BUT...
HE DOESN'T LOOK LIKE HIM AT ALL! MAYBE THAT KID IS PLAYING A TRICK ON ME!
SO, DID YOU FIND HIM?
I DON'T GET IT AT ALL... THEY TOLD ME MOZART WAS THAT MAN AT THE TABLE, BUT IT JUST DOESN'T LOOK LIKE HIM ...
BONZO, I'M GOING TO FEED YOU TO THE SHARKS*!

*I'M GOING TO PUNISH YOU!

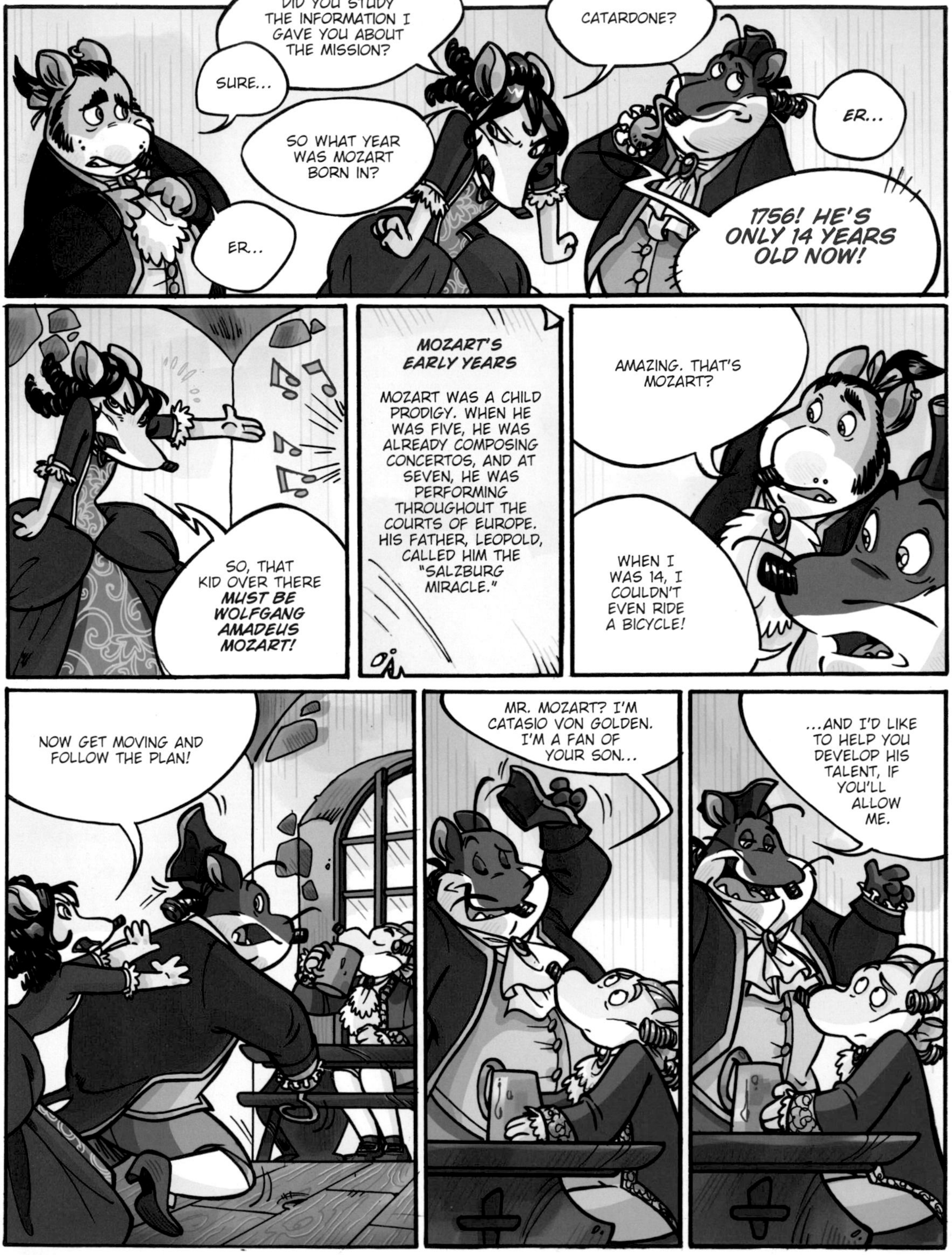

DID YOU STUDY THE INFORMATION I GAVE YOU ABOUT THE MISSION?
SURE...
CATARDONE?
SO WHAT YEAR WAS MOZART BORN IN?
ER...
ER...
1756! HE'S ONLY 14 YEARS OLD NOW!
SO, THAT KID OVER THERE MUST BE WOLFGANG AMADEUS MOZART!
MOZART'S EARLY YEARS
MOZART WAS A CHILD PRODIGY. WHEN HE WAS FIVE, HE WAS ALREADY COMPOSING CONCERTOS, AND AT SEVEN, HE WAS PERFORMING THROUGHOUT THE COURTS OF EUROPE. HIS FATHER, LEOPOLD, CALLED HIM THE "SALZBURG MIRACLE."
AMAZING. THAT'S MOZART?
WHEN I WAS 14, I COULDN'T EVEN RIDE A BICYCLE!
NOW GET MOVING AND FOLLOW THE PLAN!
MR. MOZART? I'M CATASIO VON GOLDEN. I'M A FAN OF YOUR SON...
...AND I'D LIKE TO HELP YOU DEVELOP HIS TALENT, IF YOU'LL ALLOW ME.

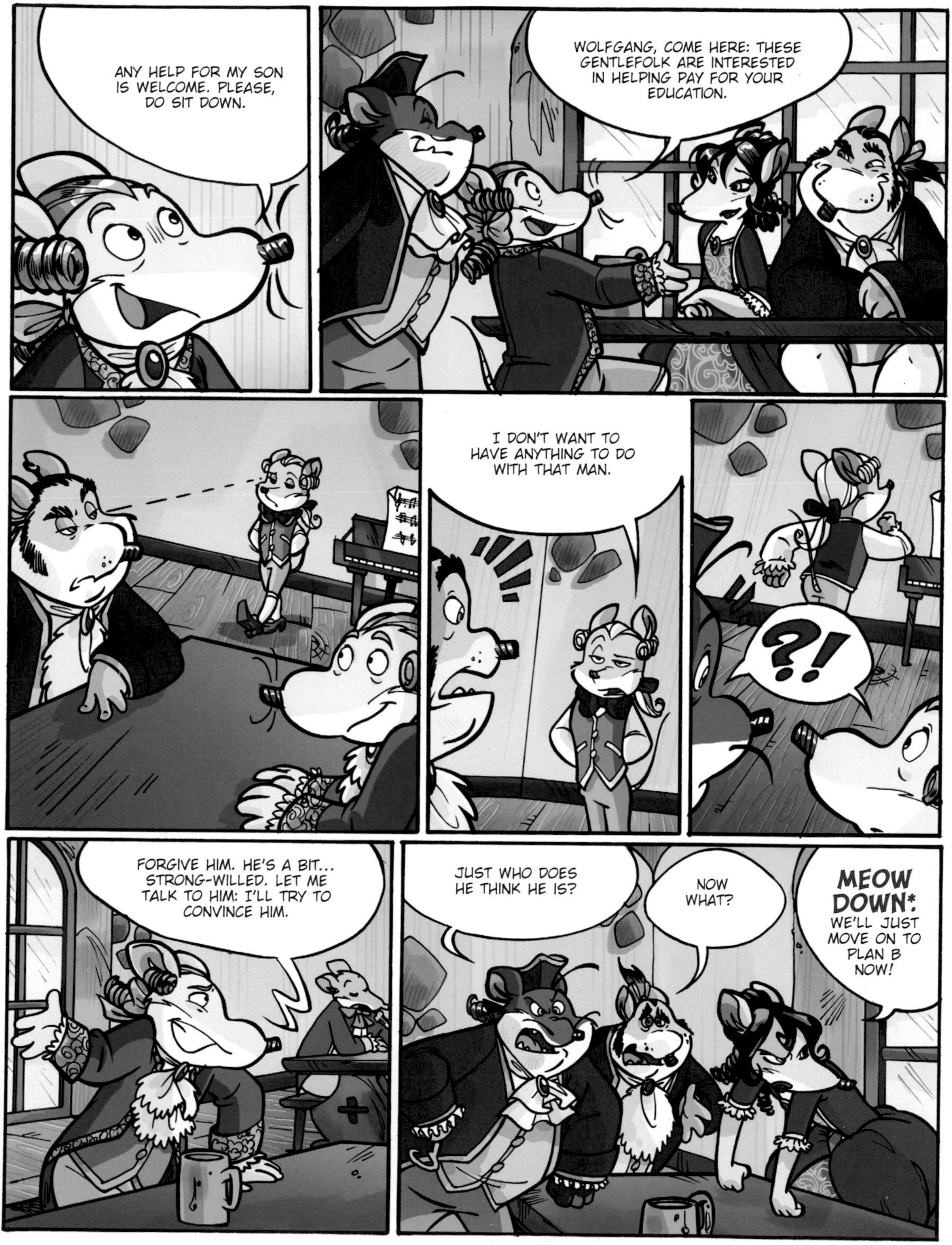
ANY HELP FOR MY SON IS WELCOME. PLEASE, DO SIT DOWN.
WOLFGANG, COME HERE: THESE GENTLEFOLK ARE INTERESTED IN HELPING PAY FOR YOUR EDUCATION.
I DON'T WANT TO HAVE ANYTHING TO DO WITH THAT MAN.
?!
FORGIVE HIM. HE'S A BIT... STRONG-WILLED. LET ME TALK TO HIM: I'LL TRY TO CONVINCE HIM.
JUST WHO DOES HE THINK HE IS?
NOW WHAT?
MEOW DOWN*. WE'LL JUST MOVE ON TO PLAN B NOW!

*CALM DOWN

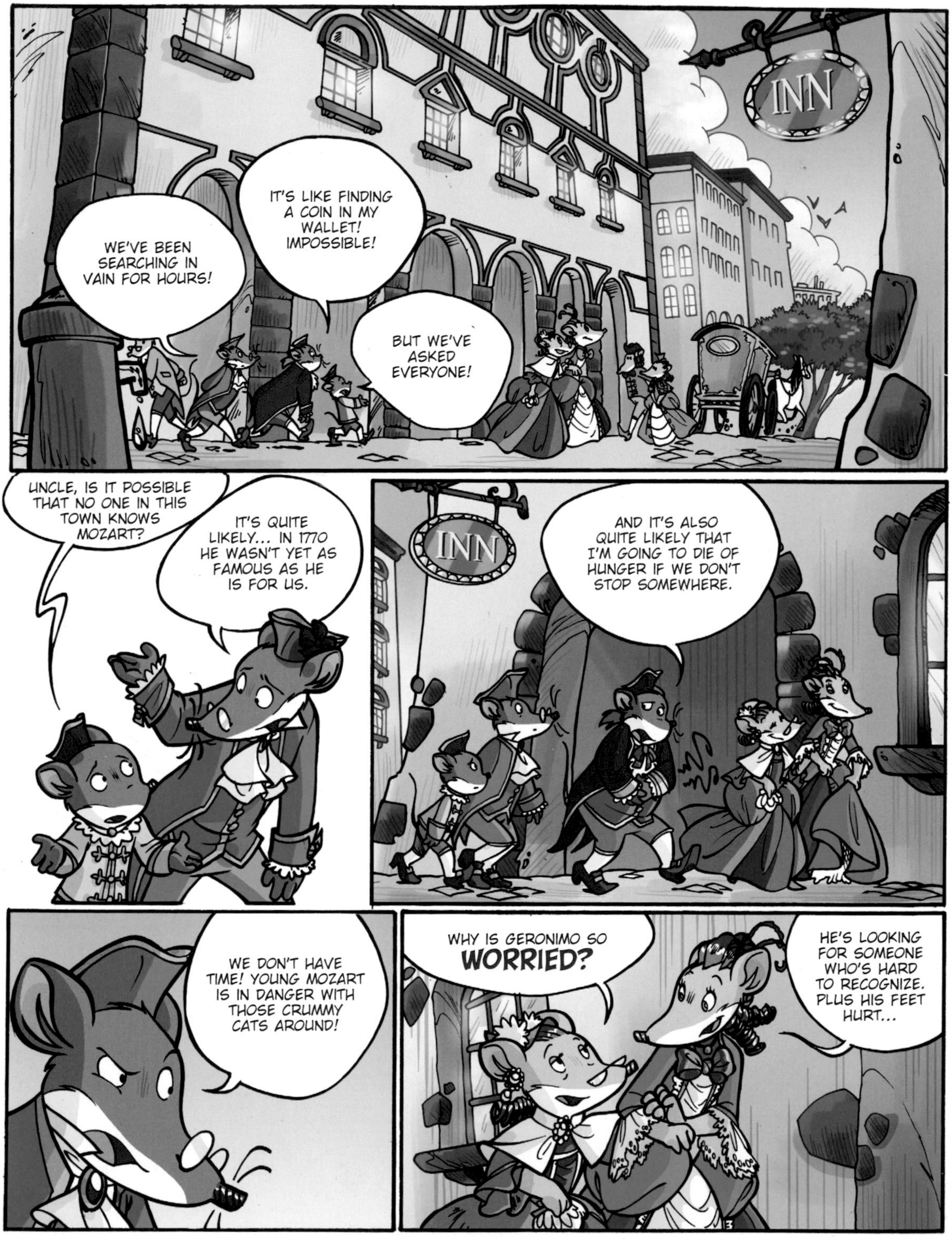
WE'VE BEEN SEARCHING IN VAIN FOR HOURS!
IT'S LIKE FINDING A COIN IN MY WALLET! IMPOSSIBLE!
BUT WE'VE ASKED EVERYONE!
INN
UNCLE, IS IT POSSIBLE THAT NO ONE IN THIS TOWN KNOWS MOZART?
IT'S QUITE LIKELY... IN 1770 HE WASN'T YET AS FAMOUS AS HE IS FOR US.
AND IT'S ALSO QUITE LIKELY THAT I'M GOING TO DIE OF HUNGER IF WE DON'T STOP SOMEWHERE.
INN
WE DON'T HAVE TIME! YOUNG MOZART IS IN DANGER WITH THOSE CRUMMY CATS AROUND!
WHY IS GERONIMO SO **WORRIED?**
HE'S LOOKING FOR SOMEONE WHO'S HARD TO RECOGNIZE. PLUS HIS FEET HURT...

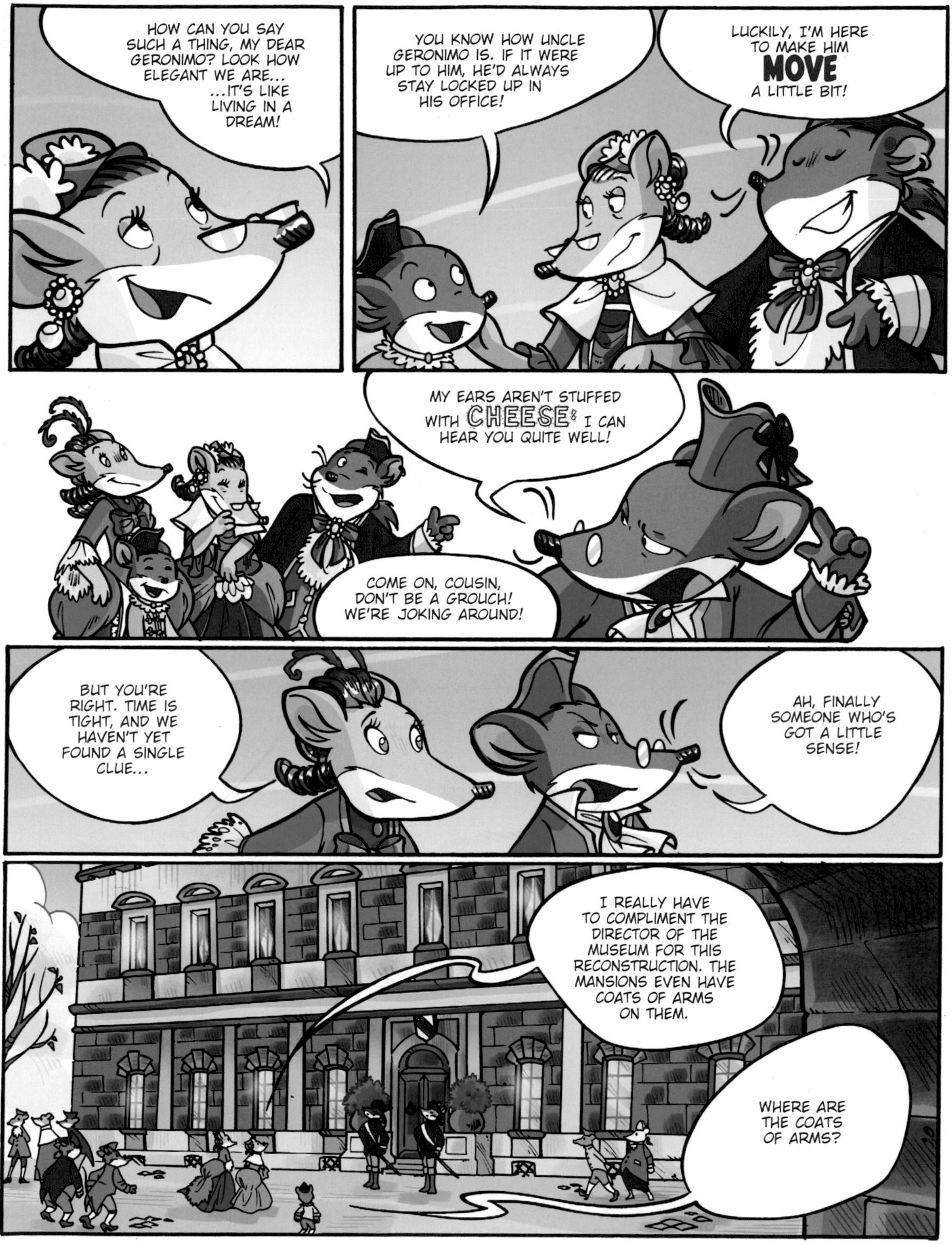
HOW CAN YOU SAY SUCH A THING, MY DEAR GERONIMO? LOOK HOW ELEGANT WE ARE...
...IT'S LIKE LIVING IN A DREAM!
YOU KNOW HOW UNCLE GERONIMO IS. IF IT WERE UP TO HIM, HE'D ALWAYS STAY LOCKED UP IN HIS OFFICE!
LUCKILY, I'M HERE TO MAKE HIM MOVE A LITTLE BIT!
MY EARS AREN'T STUFFED WITH CHEESE: I CAN HEAR YOU QUITE WELL!
COME ON, COUSIN, DON'T BE A GROUCH! WE'RE JOKING AROUND!
BUT YOU'RE RIGHT. TIME IS TIGHT, AND WE HAVEN'T YET FOUND A SINGLE CLUE...
AH, FINALLY SOMEONE WHO'S GOT A LITTLE SENSE!
I REALLY HAVE TO COMPLIMENT THE DIRECTOR OF THE MUSEUM FOR THIS RECONSTRUCTION. THE MANSIONS EVEN HAVE COATS OF ARMS ON THEM.
WHERE ARE THE COATS OF ARMS?

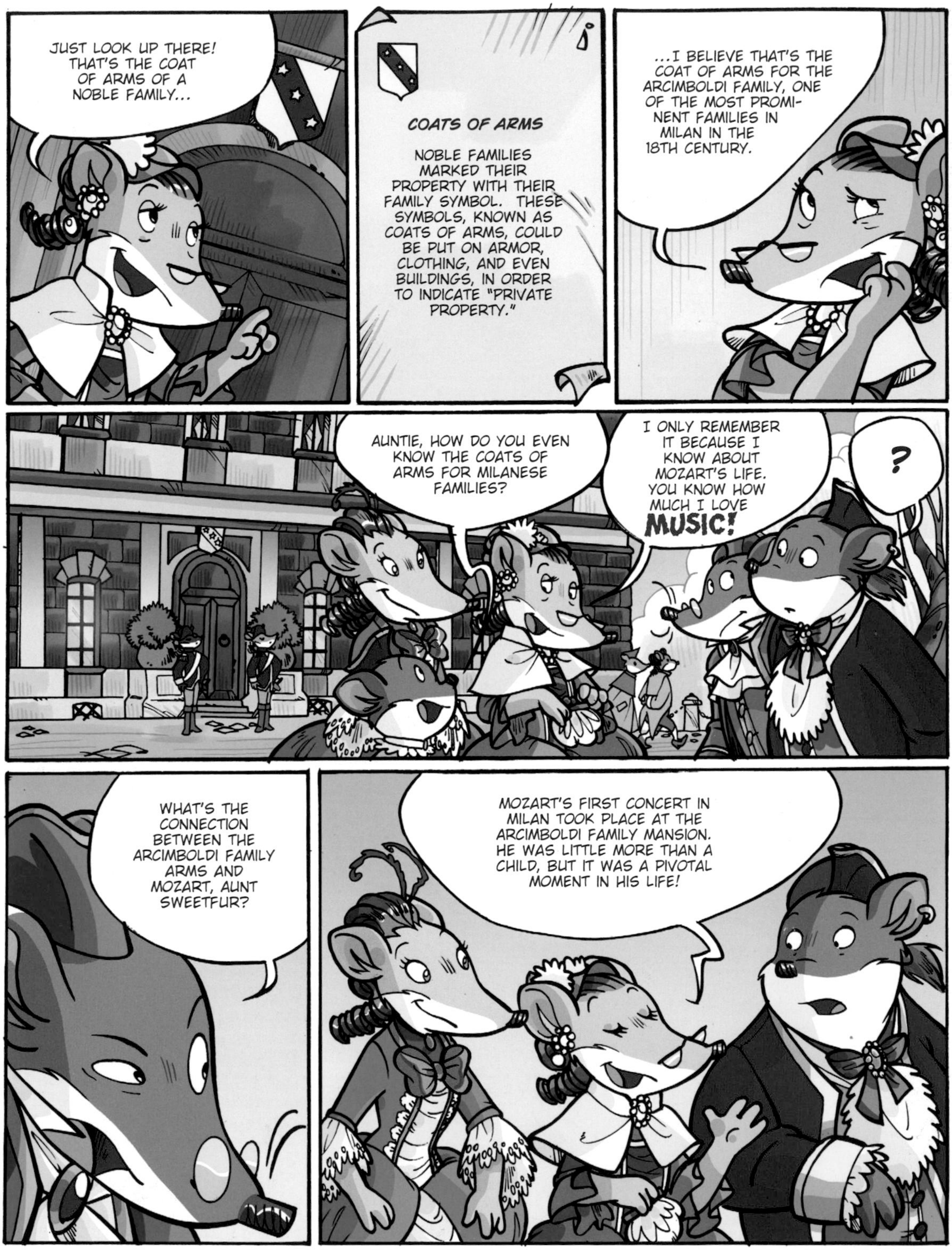
JUST LOOK UP THERE! THAT'S THE COAT OF ARMS OF A NOBLE FAMILY...
COATS OF ARMS
NOBLE FAMILIES MARKED THEIR PROPERTY WITH THEIR FAMILY SYMBOL. THESE SYMBOLS, KNOWN AS COATS OF ARMS, COULD BE PUT ON ARMOR, CLOTHING, AND EVEN BUILDINGS, IN ORDER TO INDICATE "PRIVATE PROPERTY."
...I BELIEVE THAT'S THE COAT OF ARMS FOR THE ARCIMBOLDI FAMILY, ONE OF THE MOST PROMI-NENT FAMILIES IN MILAN IN THE 18TH CENTURY.
AUNTIE, HOW DO YOU EVEN KNOW THE COATS OF ARMS FOR MILANESE FAMILIES?
I ONLY REMEMBER IT BECAUSE I KNOW ABOUT MOZART'S LIFE. YOU KNOW HOW MUCH I LOVE MUSIC!
?
WHAT'S THE CONNECTION BETWEEN THE ARCIMBOLDI FAMILY ARMS AND MOZART, AUNT SWEETFUR?
MOZART'S FIRST CONCERT IN MILAN TOOK PLACE AT THE ARCIMBOLDI FAMILY MANSION. HE WAS LITTLE MORE THAN A CHILD, BUT IT WAS A PIVOTAL MOMENT IN HIS LIFE!

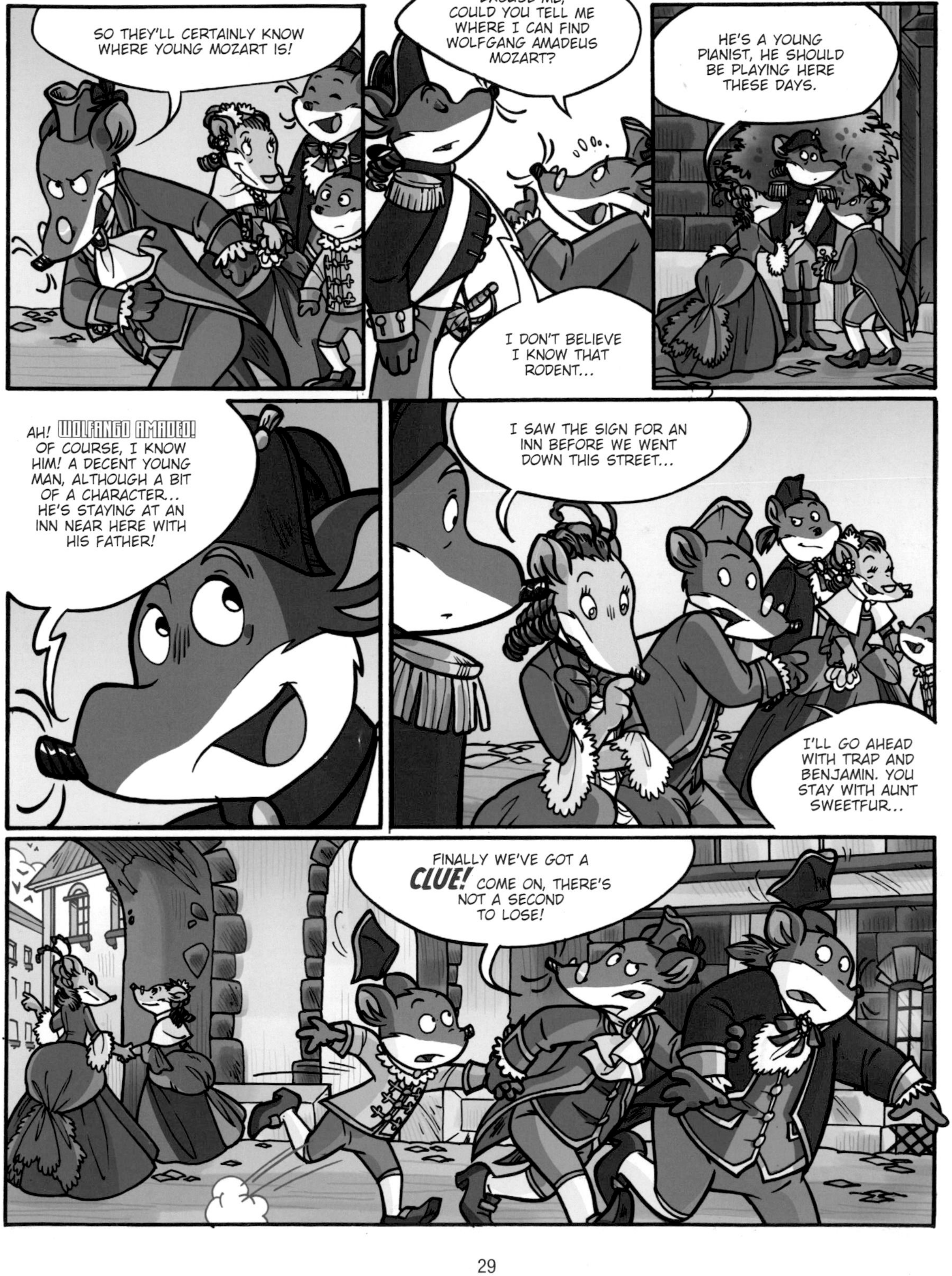
SO THEY'LL CERTAINLY KNOW WHERE YOUNG MOZART IS!
EXCUSE ME, COULD YOU TELL ME WHERE I CAN FIND WOLFGANG AMADEUS MOZART?
I DON'T BELIEVE I KNOW THAT RODENT...
HE'S A YOUNG PIANIST, HE SHOULD BE PLAYING HERE THESE DAYS.
AH! WOLFANGO AMADEO! OF COURSE, I KNOW HIM! A DECENT YOUNG MAN, ALTHOUGH A BIT OF A CHARACTER... HE'S STAYING AT AN INN NEAR HERE WITH HIS FATHER!
I SAW THE SIGN FOR AN INN BEFORE WE WENT DOWN THIS STREET...
I'LL GO AHEAD WITH TRAP AND BENJAMIN. YOU STAY WITH AUNT SWEETFUR...
FINALLY WE'VE GOT A CLUE! COME ON, THERE'S NOT A SECOND TO LOSE!

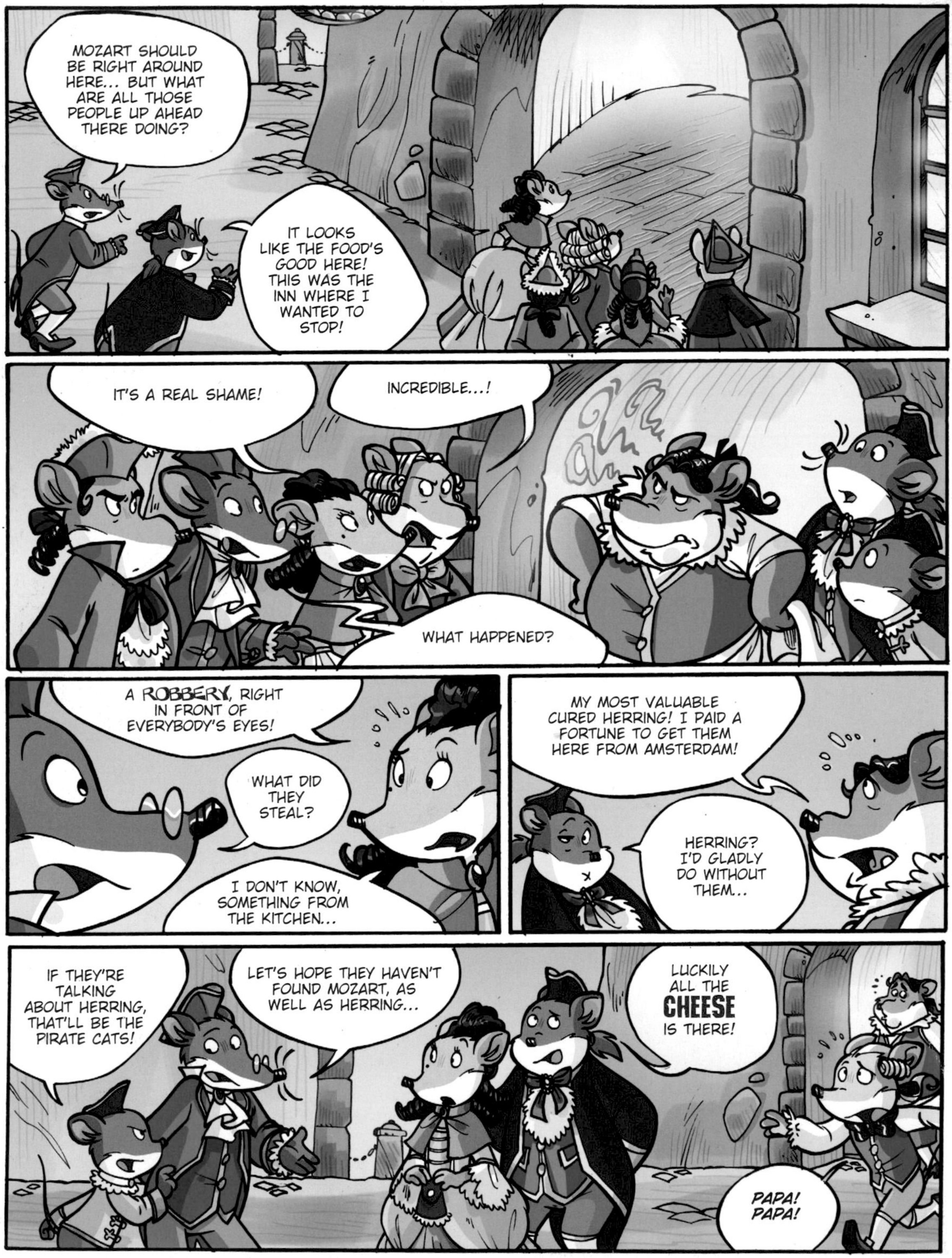
MOZART SHOULD BE RIGHT AROUND HERE... BUT WHAT ARE ALL THOSE PEOPLE UP AHEAD THERE DOING?
IT LOOKS LIKE THE FOOD'S GOOD HERE! THIS WAS THE INN WHERE I WANTED TO STOP!
IT'S A REAL SHAME!
INCREDIBLE...!
WHAT HAPPENED?
A ROBBERY, RIGHT IN FRONT OF EVERYBODY'S EYES!
WHAT DID THEY STEAL?
I DON'T KNOW, SOMETHING FROM THE KITCHEN...
MY MOST VALUABLE CURED HERRING! I PAID A FORTUNE TO GET THEM HERE FROM AMSTERDAM!
HERRING? I'D GLADLY DO WITHOUT THEM...
IF THEY'RE TALKING ABOUT HERRING, THAT'LL BE THE PIRATE CATS!
LET'S HOPE THEY HAVEN'T FOUND MOZART, AS WELL AS HERRING...
LUCKILY ALL THE CHEESE IS THERE!
PAPA! PAPA!

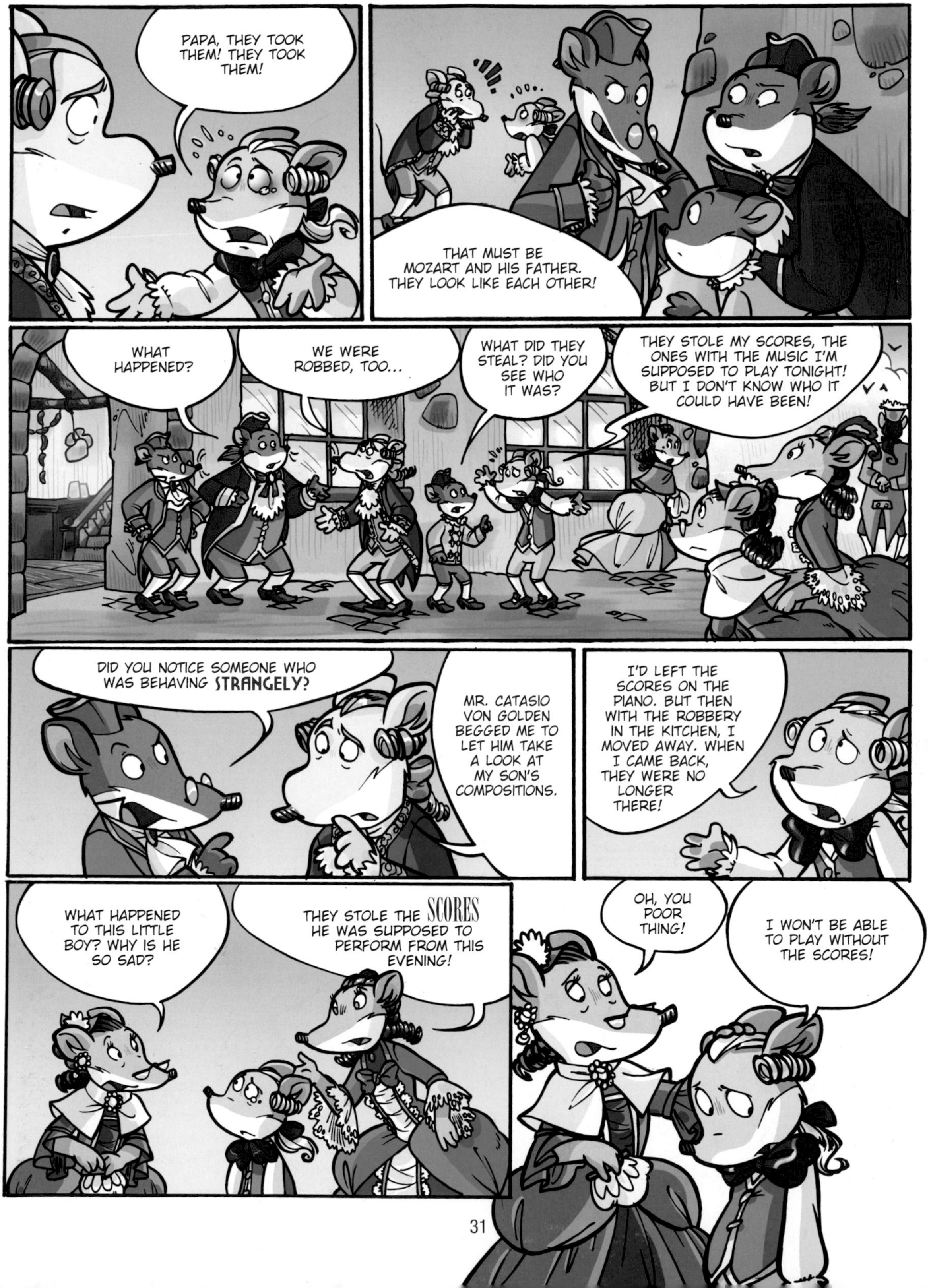
PAPA, THEY TOOK THEM! THEY TOOK THEM!
THAT MUST BE MOZART AND HIS FATHER. THEY LOOK LIKE EACH OTHER!
WHAT HAPPENED?
WE WERE ROBBED, TOO...
WHAT DID THEY STEAL? DID YOU SEE WHO IT WAS?
THEY STOLE MY SCORES, THE ONES WITH THE MUSIC I'M SUPPOSED TO PLAY TONIGHT! BUT I DON'T KNOW WHO IT COULD HAVE BEEN!
DID YOU NOTICE SOMEONE WHO WAS BEHAVING STRANGELY?
MR. CATASIO VON GOLDEN BEGGED ME TO LET HIM TAKE A LOOK AT MY SON'S COMPOSITIONS.
I'D LEFT THE SCORES ON THE PIANO. BUT THEN WITH THE ROBBERY IN THE KITCHEN, I MOVED AWAY. WHEN I CAME BACK, THEY WERE NO LONGER THERE!
WHAT HAPPENED TO THIS LITTLE BOY? WHY IS HE SO SAD?
THEY STOLE THE SCORES HE WAS SUPPOSED TO PERFORM FROM THIS EVENING!
OH, YOU POOR THING!
I WON'T BE ABLE TO PLAY WITHOUT THE SCORES!

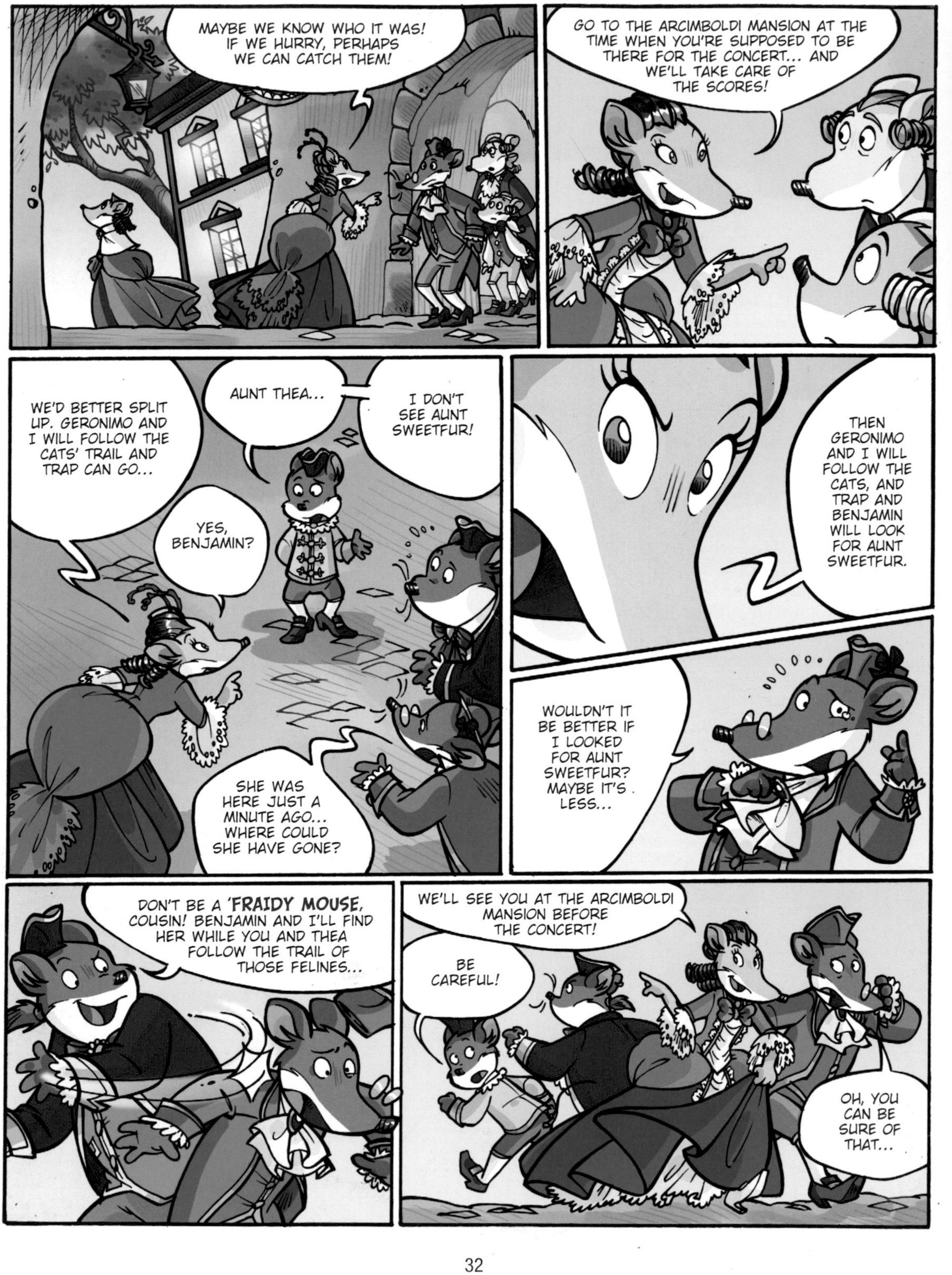
MAYBE WE KNOW WHO IT WAS! IF WE HURRY, PERHAPS WE CAN CATCH THEM!
GO TO THE ARCIMBOLDI MANSION AT THE TIME WHEN YOU'RE SUPPOSED TO BE THERE FOR THE CONCERT... AND WE'LL TAKE CARE OF THE SCORES!
WE'D BETTER SPLIT UP. GERONIMO AND I WILL FOLLOW THE CATS' TRAIL AND TRAP CAN GO...
AUNT THEA...
I DON'T SEE AUNT SWEETFUR!
YES, BENJAMIN?
SHE WAS HERE JUST A MINUTE AGO... WHERE COULD SHE HAVE GONE?
THEN GERONIMO AND I WILL FOLLOW THE CATS, AND TRAP AND BENJAMIN WILL LOOK FOR AUNT SWEETFUR.
WOULDN'T IT BE BETTER IF I LOOKED FOR AUNT SWEETFUR? MAYBE IT'S LESS...
DON'T BE A 'FRAIDY MOUSE, COUSIN! BENJAMIN AND I'LL FIND HER WHILE YOU AND THEA FOLLOW THE TRAIL OF THOSE FELINES...
WE'LL SEE YOU AT THE ARCIMBOLDI MANSION BEFORE THE CONCERT!
BE CAREFUL!
OH, YOU CAN BE SURE OF THAT...

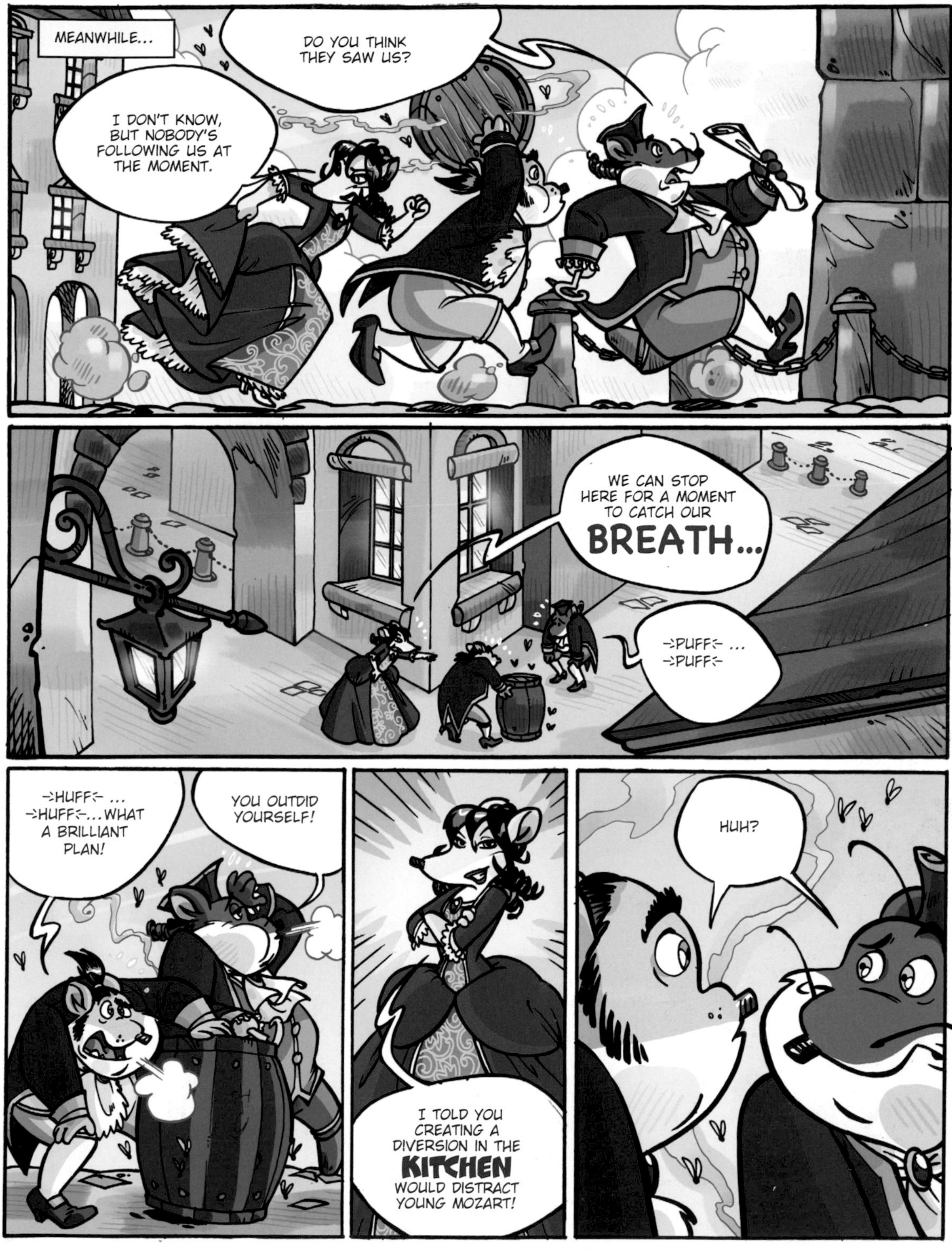
MEANWHILE...
DO YOU THINK THEY SAW US?
I DON'T KNOW, BUT NOBODY'S FOLLOWING US AT THE MOMENT.
WE CAN STOP HERE FOR A MOMENT TO CATCH OUR BREATH...
-PUFF- ... -PUFF-
-HUFF- ... -HUFF-...WHAT A BRILLIANT PLAN!
YOU OUTDID YOURSELF!
I TOLD YOU CREATING A DIVERSION IN THE KITCHEN WOULD DISTRACT YOUNG MOZART!
HUH?

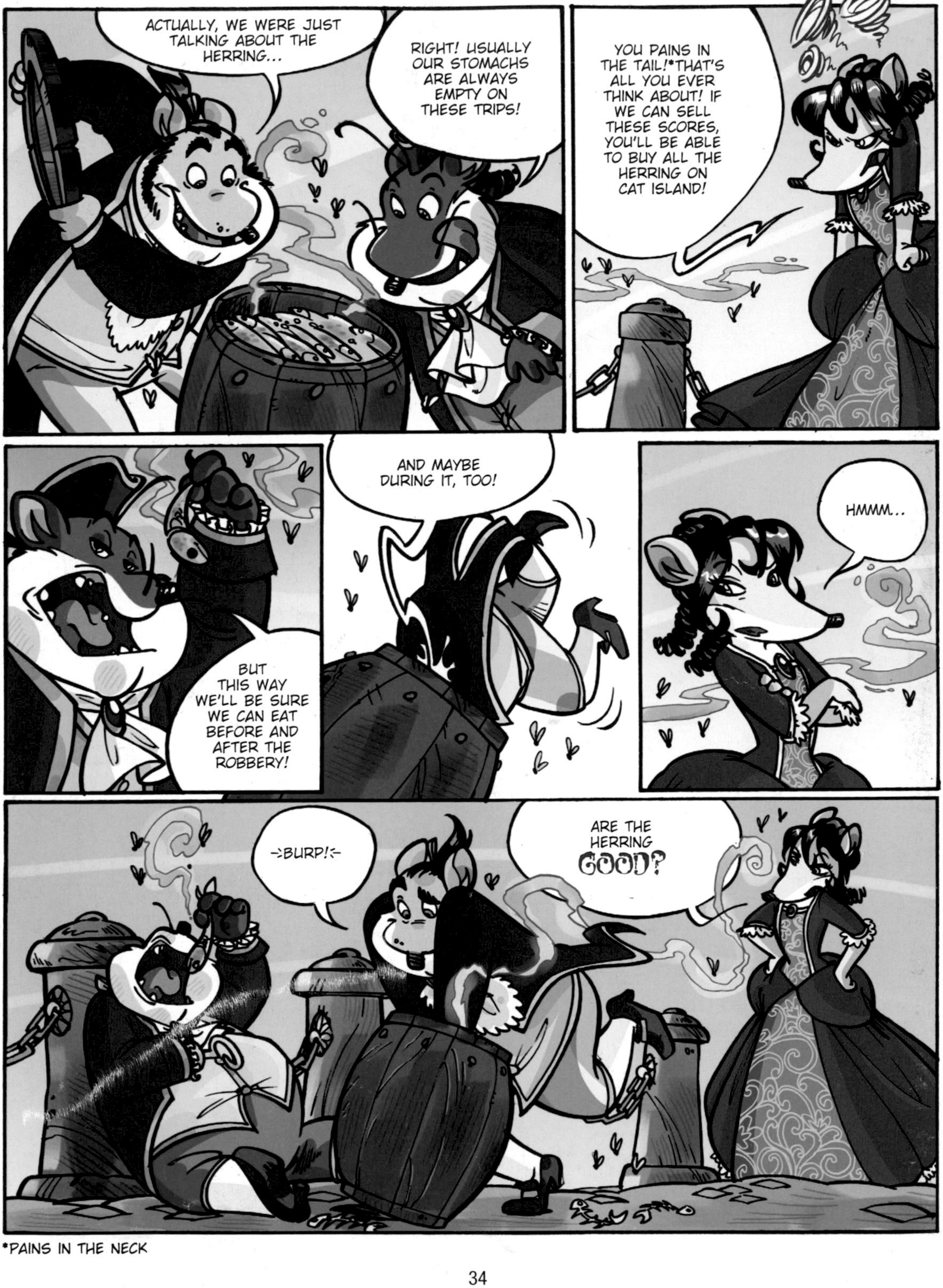
ACTUALLY, WE WERE JUST TALKING ABOUT THE HERRING...
RIGHT! USUALLY OUR STOMACHS ARE ALWAYS EMPTY ON THESE TRIPS!
YOU PAINS IN THE TAIL!*THAT'S ALL YOU EVER THINK ABOUT! IF WE CAN SELL THESE SCORES, YOU'LL BE ABLE TO BUY ALL THE HERRING ON CAT ISLAND!
BUT THIS WAY WE'LL BE SURE WE CAN EAT BEFORE AND AFTER THE ROBBERY!
AND MAYBE DURING IT, TOO!
HMMM...
-BURP!-
ARE THE HERRING GOOD?

*PAINS IN THE NECK

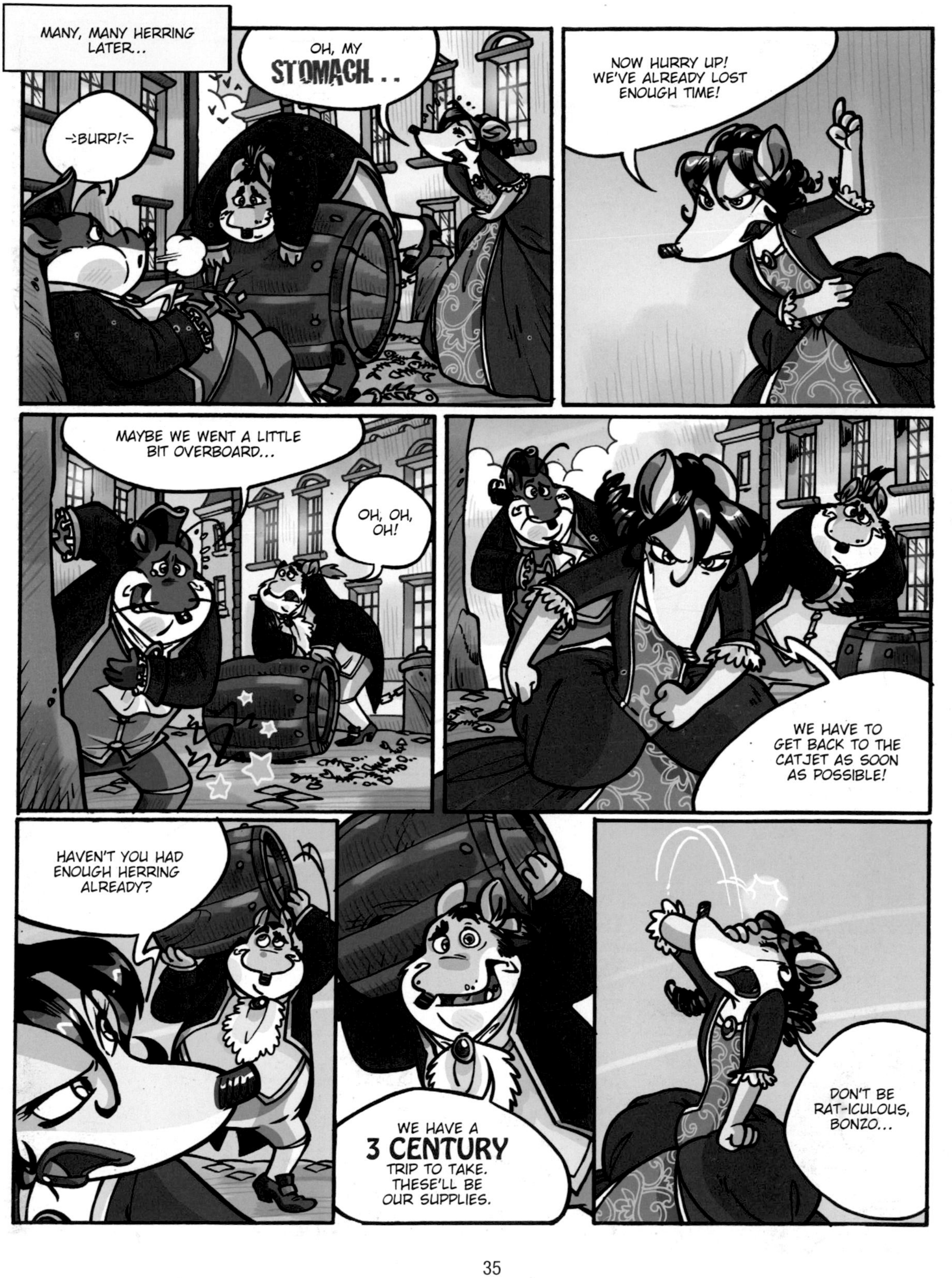
MANY, MANY HERRING LATER...
-BURP!-
OH, MY STOMACH...
NOW HURRY UP! WE'VE ALREADY LOST ENOUGH TIME!
MAYBE WE WENT A LITTLE BIT OVERBOARD...
OH, OH, OH!
WE HAVE TO GET BACK TO THE CATJET AS SOON AS POSSIBLE!
HAVEN'T YOU HAD ENOUGH HERRING ALREADY?
WE HAVE A 3 CENTURY TRIP TO TAKE. THESE'LL BE OUR SUPPLIES.
DON'T BE RAT-ICULOUS, BONZO...

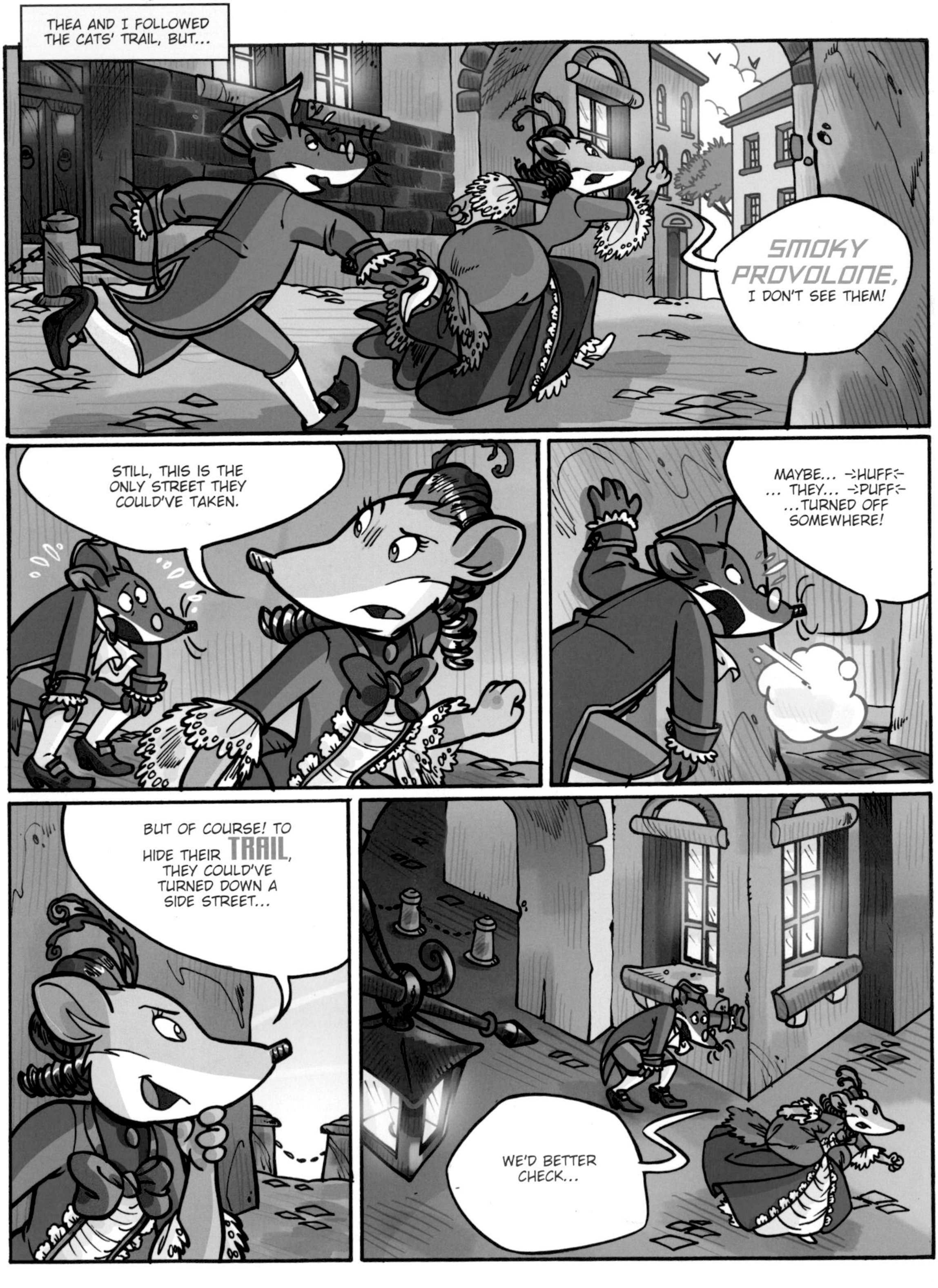

THEA AND I FOLLOWED THE CATS' TRAIL, BUT...
SMOKY PROVOLONE, I DON'T SEE THEM!
STILL, THIS IS THE ONLY STREET THEY COULD'VE TAKEN.
MAYBE... ~HUFF~ ... THEY... ~PUFF~ ...TURNED OFF SOMEWHERE!
BUT OF COURSE! TO HIDE THEIR TRAIL, THEY COULD'VE TURNED DOWN A SIDE STREET...
WE'D BETTER CHECK...

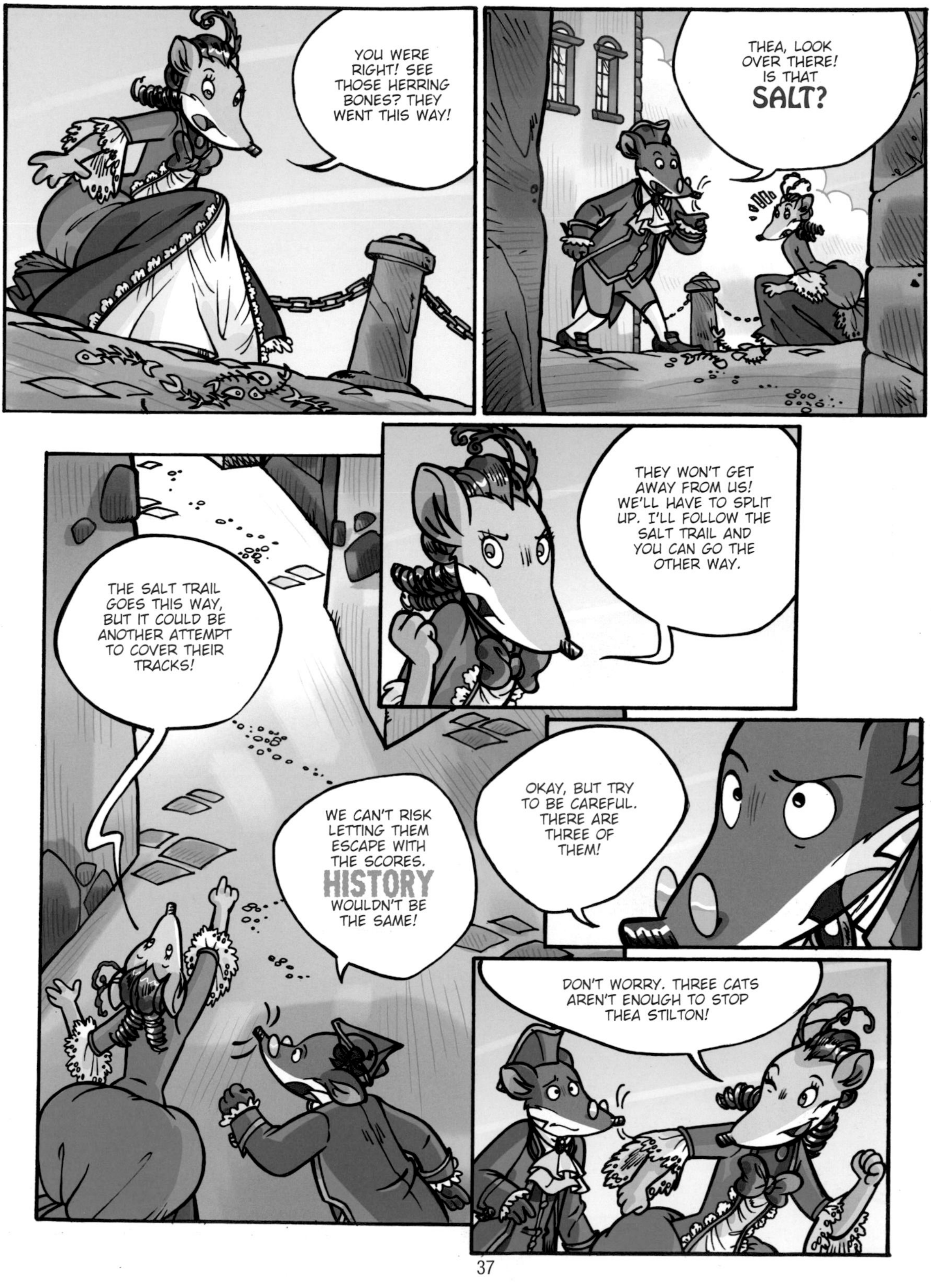

YOU WERE RIGHT! SEE THOSE HERRING BONES? THEY WENT THIS WAY!
THEA, LOOK OVER THERE! IS THAT SALT?
THEY WON'T GET AWAY FROM US! WE'LL HAVE TO SPLIT UP. I'LL FOLLOW THE SALT TRAIL AND YOU CAN GO THE OTHER WAY.
THE SALT TRAIL GOES THIS WAY, BUT IT COULD BE ANOTHER ATTEMPT TO COVER THEIR TRACKS!
WE CAN'T RISK LETTING THEM ESCAPE WITH THE SCORES. HISTORY WOULDN'T BE THE SAME!
OKAY, BUT TRY TO BE CAREFUL. THERE ARE THREE OF THEM!
DON'T WORRY. THREE CATS AREN'T ENOUGH TO STOP THEA STILTON!

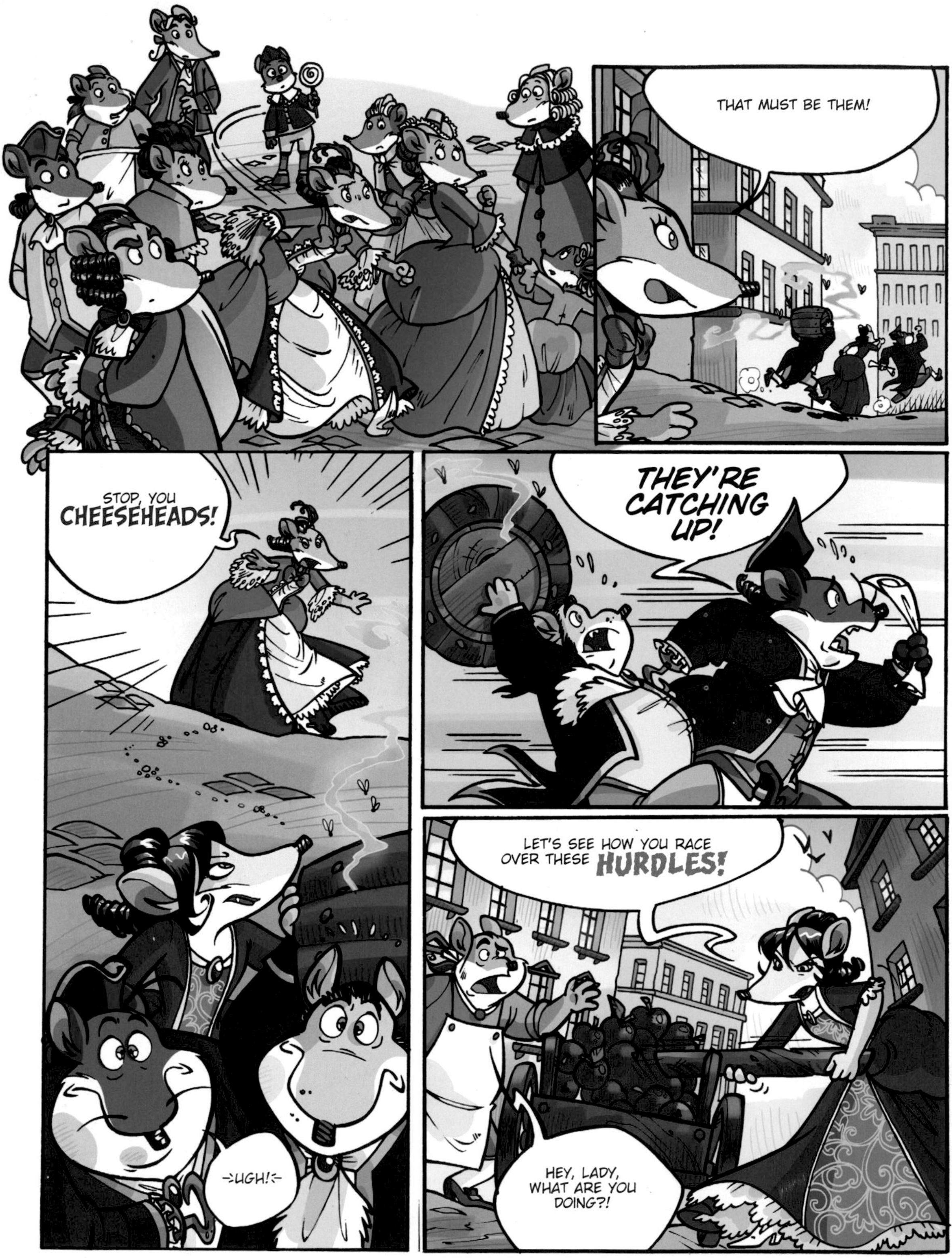
THAT MUST BE THEM!
STOP, YOU CHEESEHEADS!
THEY'RE CATCHING UP!
~UGH!~
LET'S SEE HOW YOU RACE OVER THESE HURDLES!
HEY, LADY, WHAT ARE YOU DOING?!

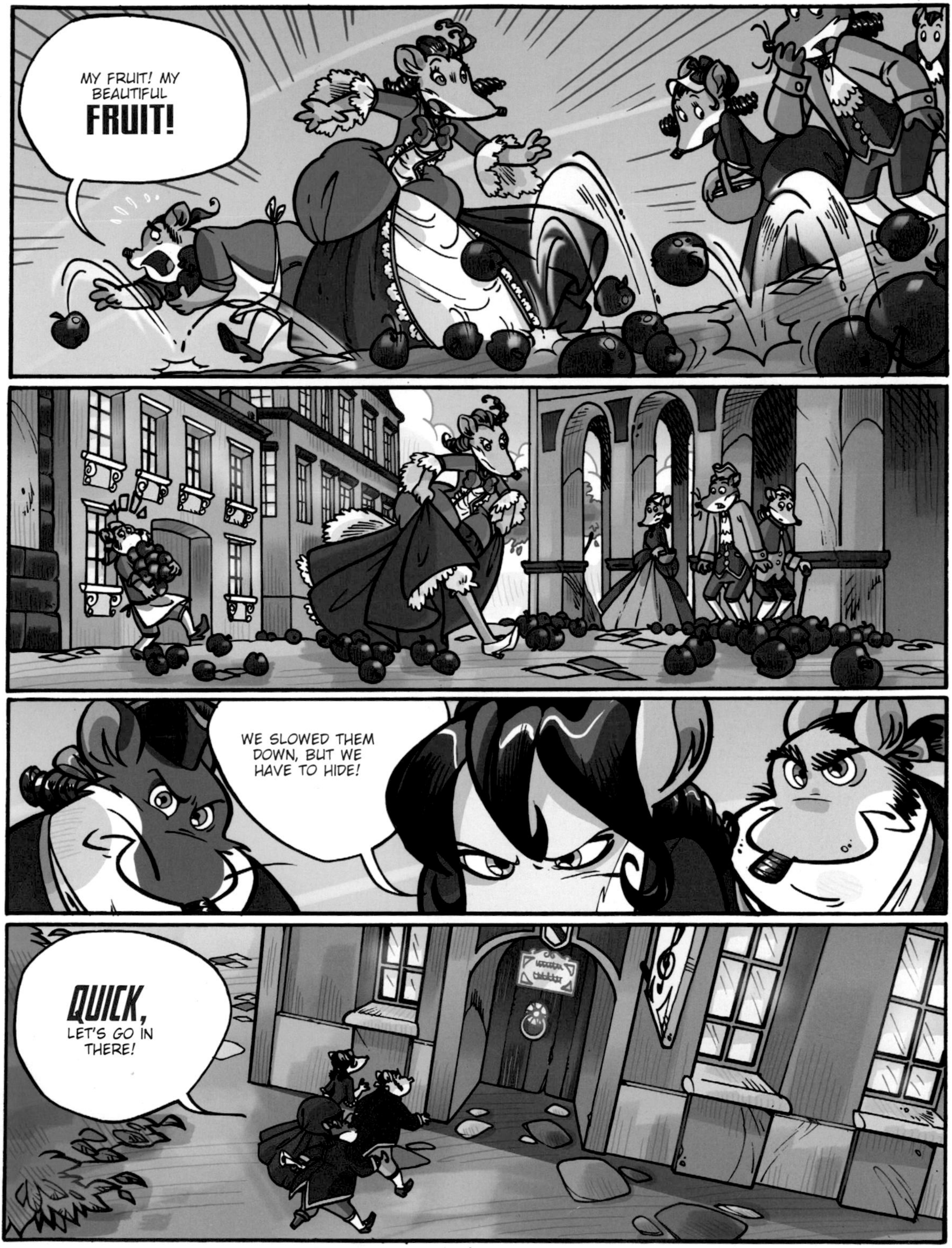

MY FRUIT! MY BEAUTIFUL FRUIT!
WE SLOWED THEM DOWN, BUT WE HAVE TO HIDE!
QUICK, LET'S GO IN THERE!

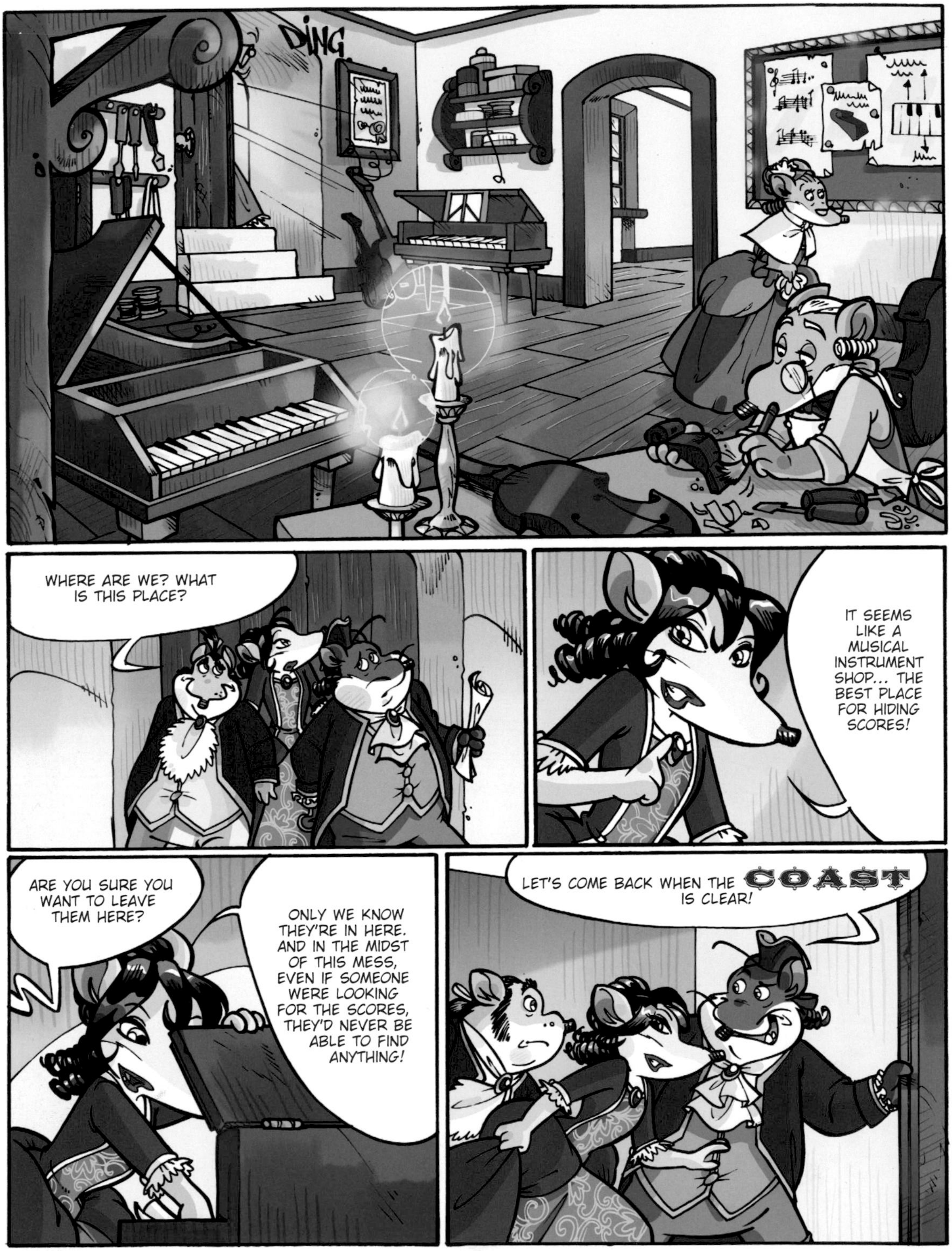
DING
WHERE ARE WE? WHAT IS THIS PLACE?
IT SEEMS LIKE A MUSICAL INSTRUMENT SHOP... THE BEST PLACE FOR HIDING SCORES!
ARE YOU SURE YOU WANT TO LEAVE THEM HERE?
ONLY WE KNOW THEY'RE IN HERE. AND IN THE MIDST OF THIS MESS, EVEN IF SOMEONE WERE LOOKING FOR THE SCORES, THEY'D NEVER BE ABLE TO FIND ANYTHING!
LET'S COME BACK WHEN THE COAST IS CLEAR!

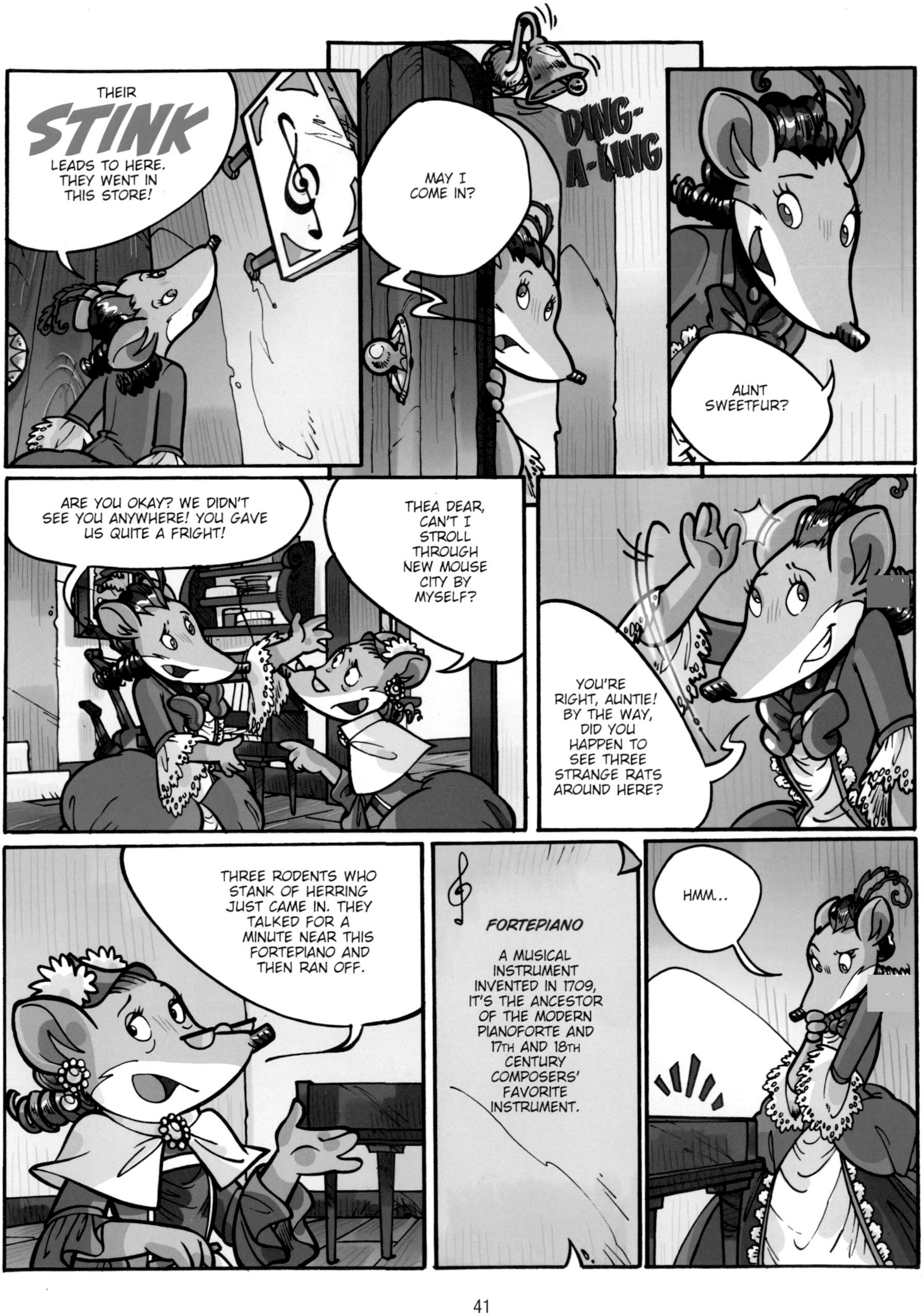

THEIR STINK LEADS TO HERE. THEY WENT IN THIS STORE!
DING-A-LING
MAY I COME IN?
AUNT SWEETFUR?
ARE YOU OKAY? WE DIDN'T SEE YOU ANYWHERE! YOU GAVE US QUITE A FRIGHT!
THEA DEAR, CAN'T I STROLL THROUGH NEW MOUSE CITY BY MYSELF?
YOU'RE RIGHT, AUNTIE! BY THE WAY, DID YOU HAPPEN TO SEE THREE STRANGE RATS AROUND HERE?
THREE RODENTS WHO STANK OF HERRING JUST CAME IN. THEY TALKED FOR A MINUTE NEAR THIS FORTEPIANO AND THEN RAN OFF.
FORTEPIANO
A MUSICAL INSTRUMENT INVENTED IN 1709, IT'S THE ANCESTOR OF THE MODERN PIANOFORTE AND 17TH AND 18TH CENTURY COMPOSERS' FAVORITE INSTRUMENT.
HMM...

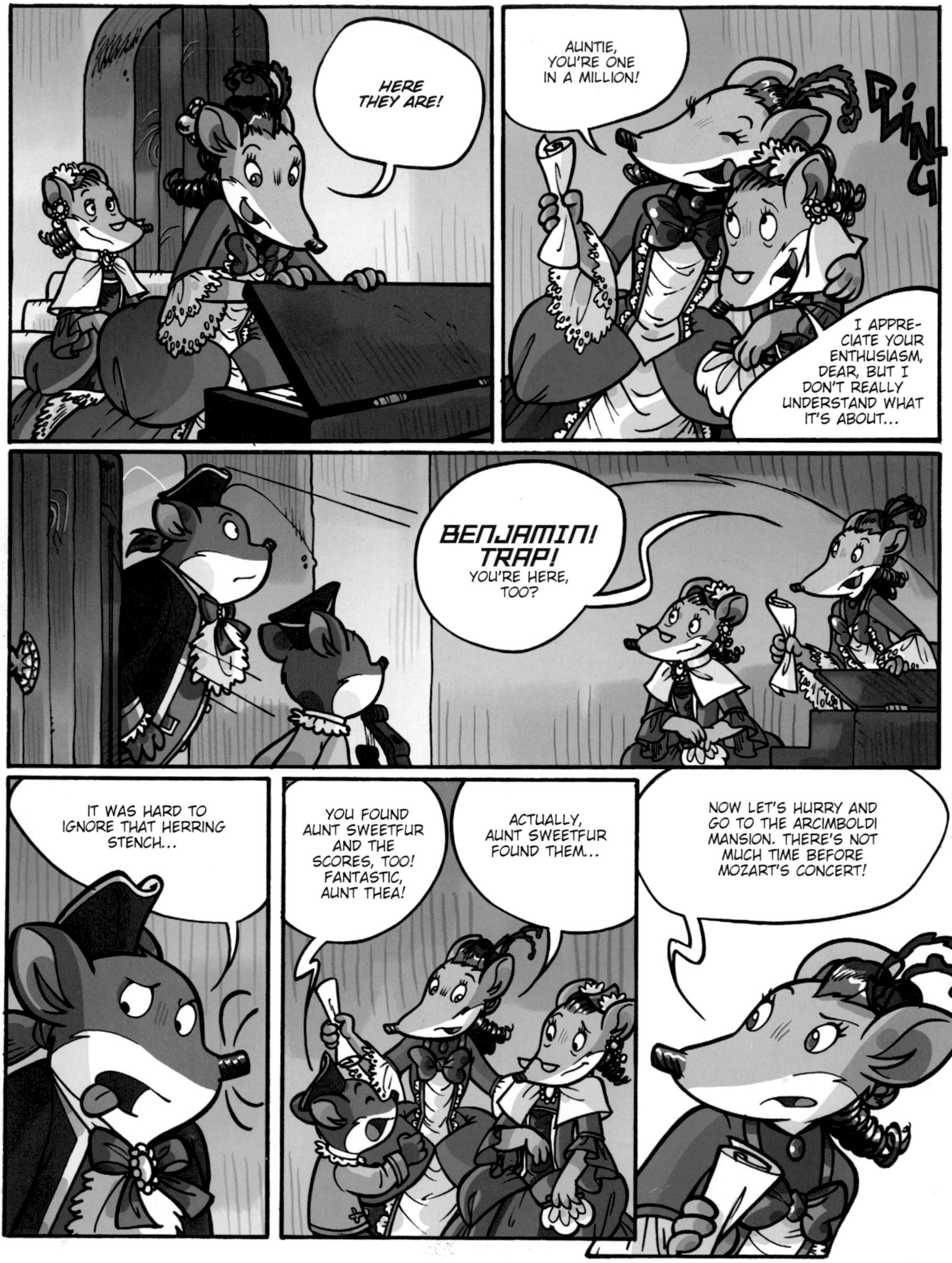
HERE THEY ARE!
AUNTIE, YOU'RE ONE IN A MILLION!
DING
I APPRECIATE YOUR ENTHUSIASM, DEAR, BUT I DON'T REALLY UNDERSTAND WHAT IT'S ABOUT...
BENJAMIN! TRAP! YOU'RE HERE, TOO?
IT WAS HARD TO IGNORE THAT HERRING STENCH...
YOU FOUND AUNT SWEETFUR AND THE SCORES, TOO! FANTASTIC, AUNT THEA!
ACTUALLY, AUNT SWEETFUR FOUND THEM...
NOW LET'S HURRY AND GO TO THE ARCIMBOLDI MANSION. THERE'S NOT MUCH TIME BEFORE MOZART'S CONCERT!

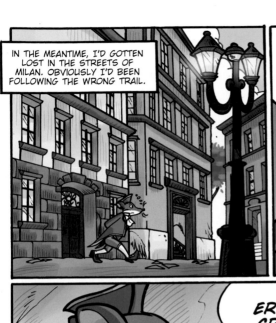

IN THE MEANTIME, I'D GOTTEN LOST IN THE STREETS OF MILAN. OBVIOUSLY I'D BEEN FOLLOWING THE WRONG TRAIL.

I'D BETTER GET BACK TO THE ARCIMBOLDI MANSION. LET'S HOPE THEA'S BEEN LUCKIER THAN ME!

BUT THEY...!

ER... STOP, YOU CRUMMY CATS!

FANCY WHO THAT IS... THAT LOUSY RAT, GERONIMO STILTON!

LET'S GET HIM!

HELP!

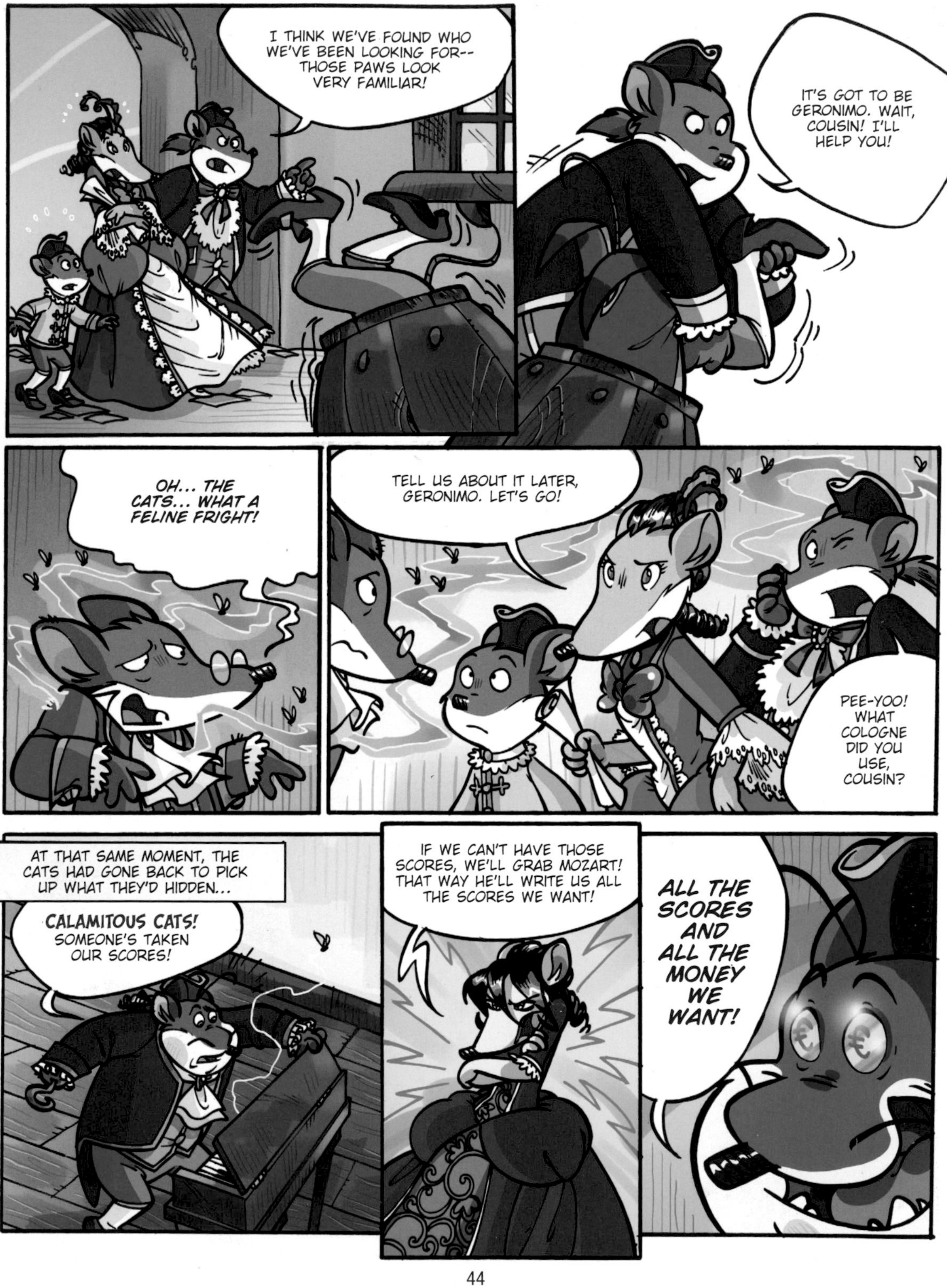
I THINK WE'VE FOUND WHO WE'VE BEEN LOOKING FOR-- THOSE PAWS LOOK VERY FAMILIAR!
IT'S GOT TO BE GERONIMO. WAIT, COUSIN! I'LL HELP YOU!
OH... THE CATS... WHAT A FELINE FRIGHT!
TELL US ABOUT IT LATER, GERONIMO. LET'S GO!
PEE-YOO! WHAT COLOGNE DID YOU USE, COUSIN?
AT THAT SAME MOMENT, THE CATS HAD GONE BACK TO PICK UP WHAT THEY'D HIDDEN...
CALAMITOUS CATS! SOMEONE'S TAKEN OUR SCORES!
IF WE CAN'T HAVE THOSE SCORES, WE'LL GRAB MOZART! THAT WAY HE'LL WRITE US ALL THE SCORES WE WANT!
ALL THE SCORES AND ALL THE MONEY WE WANT!

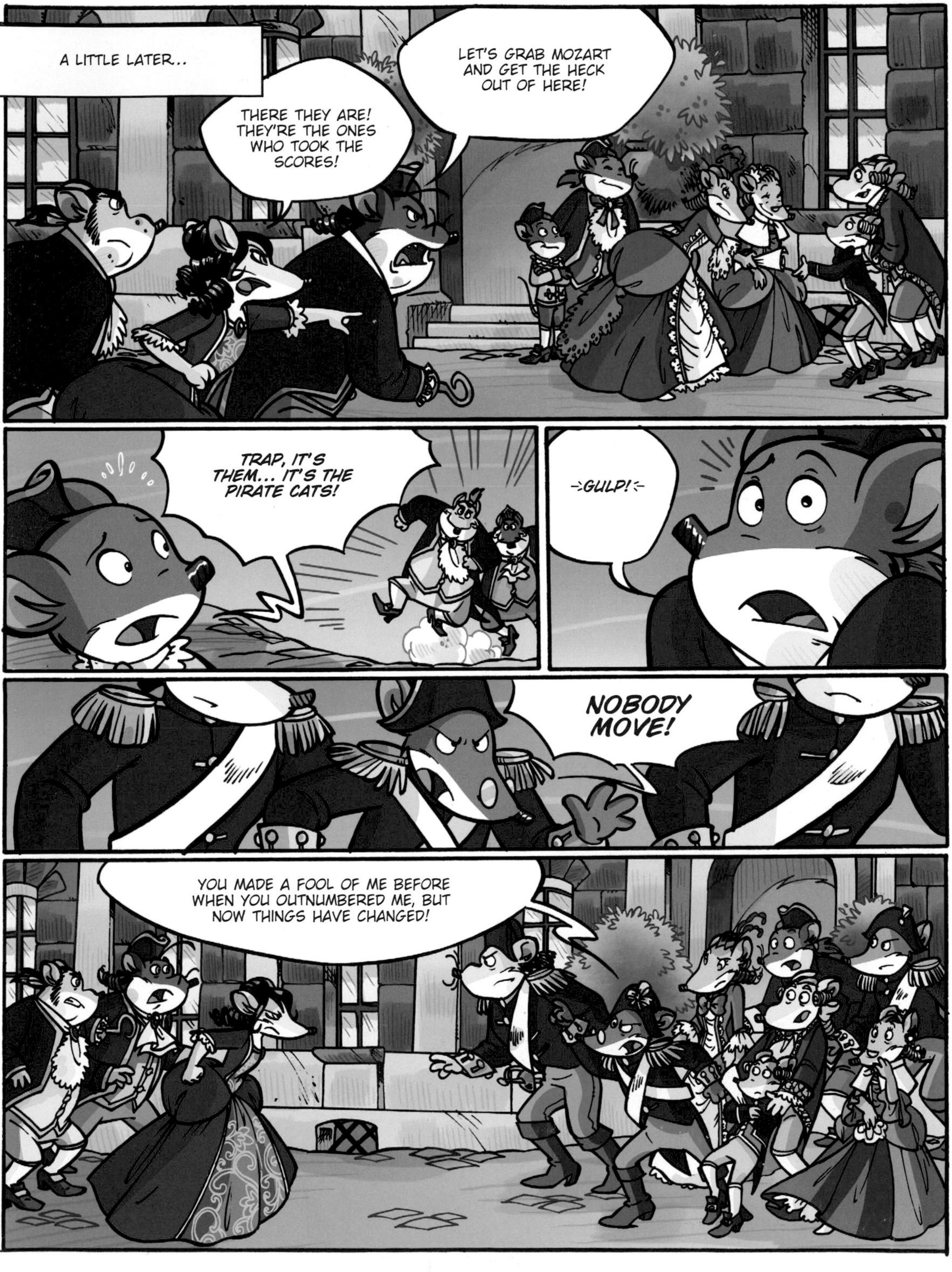
A LITTLE LATER...
THERE THEY ARE! THEY'RE THE ONES WHO TOOK THE SCORES!
LET'S GRAB MOZART AND GET THE HECK OUT OF HERE!
TRAP, IT'S THEM... IT'S THE PIRATE CATS!
GULP!
NOBODY MOVE!
YOU MADE A FOOL OF ME BEFORE WHEN YOU OUTNUMBERED ME, BUT NOW THINGS HAVE CHANGED!

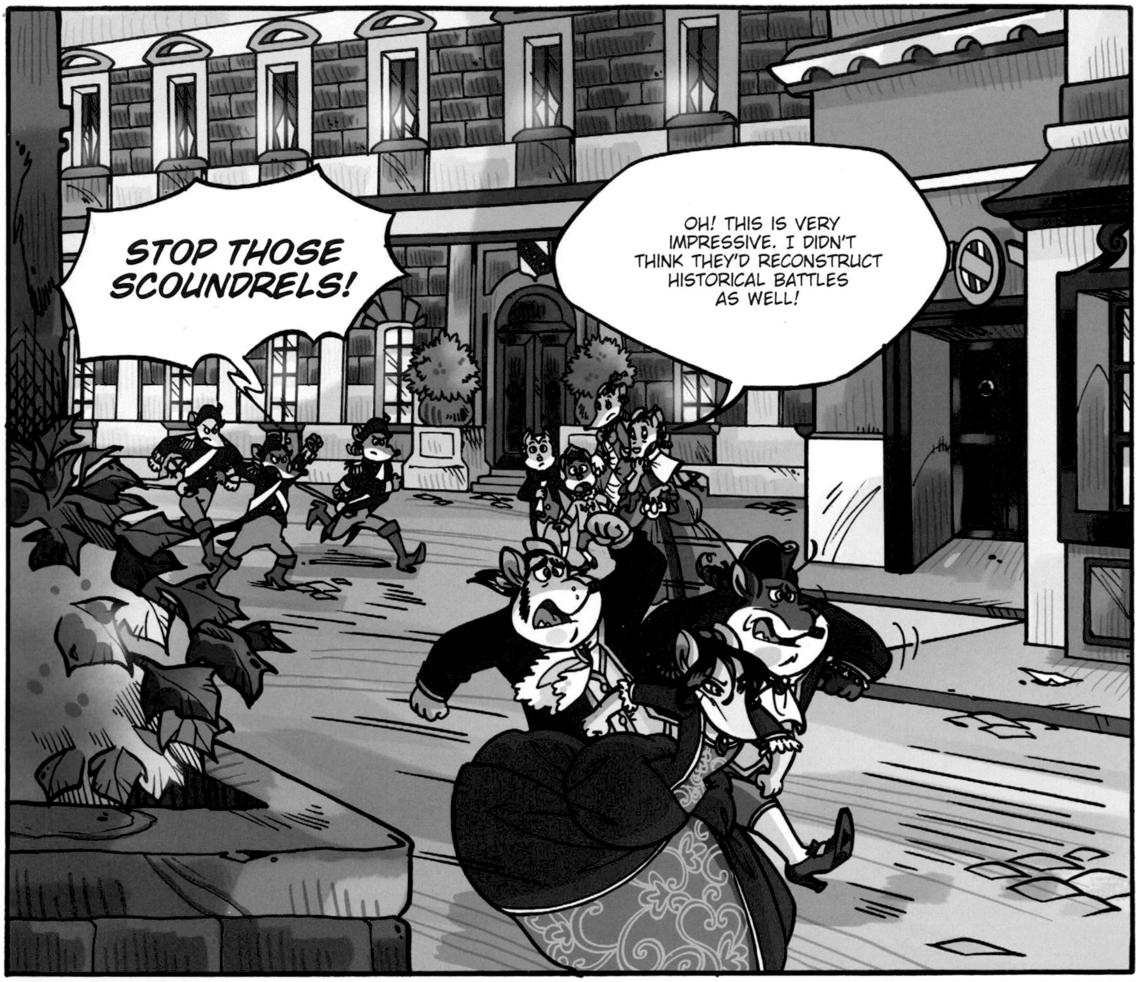
STOP THOSE SCOUNDRELS!
OH! THIS IS VERY IMPRESSIVE. I DIDN'T THINK THEY'D RECONSTRUCT HISTORICAL BATTLES AS WELL!

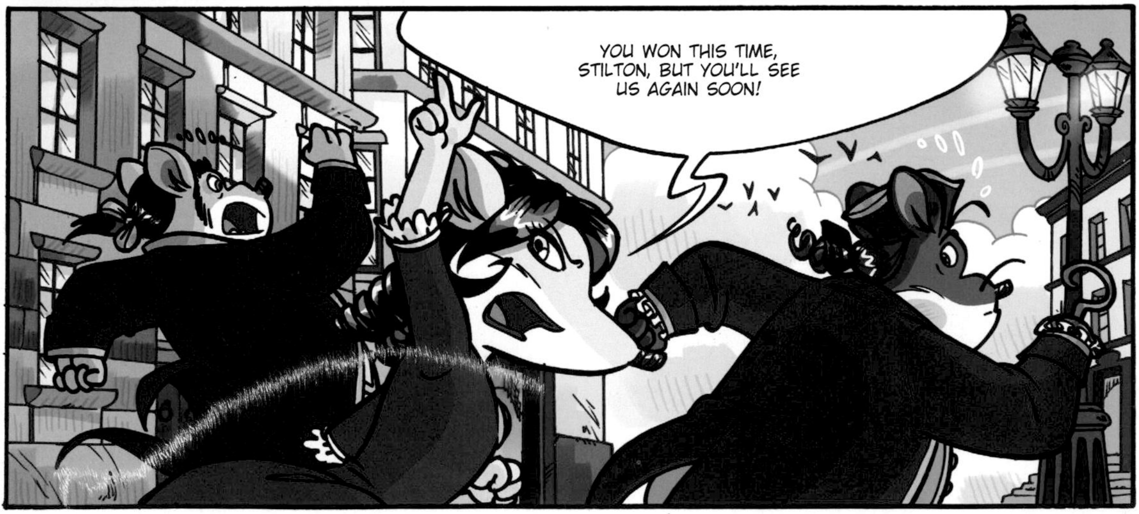
YOU WON THIS TIME, STILTON, BUT YOU'LL SEE US AGAIN SOON!

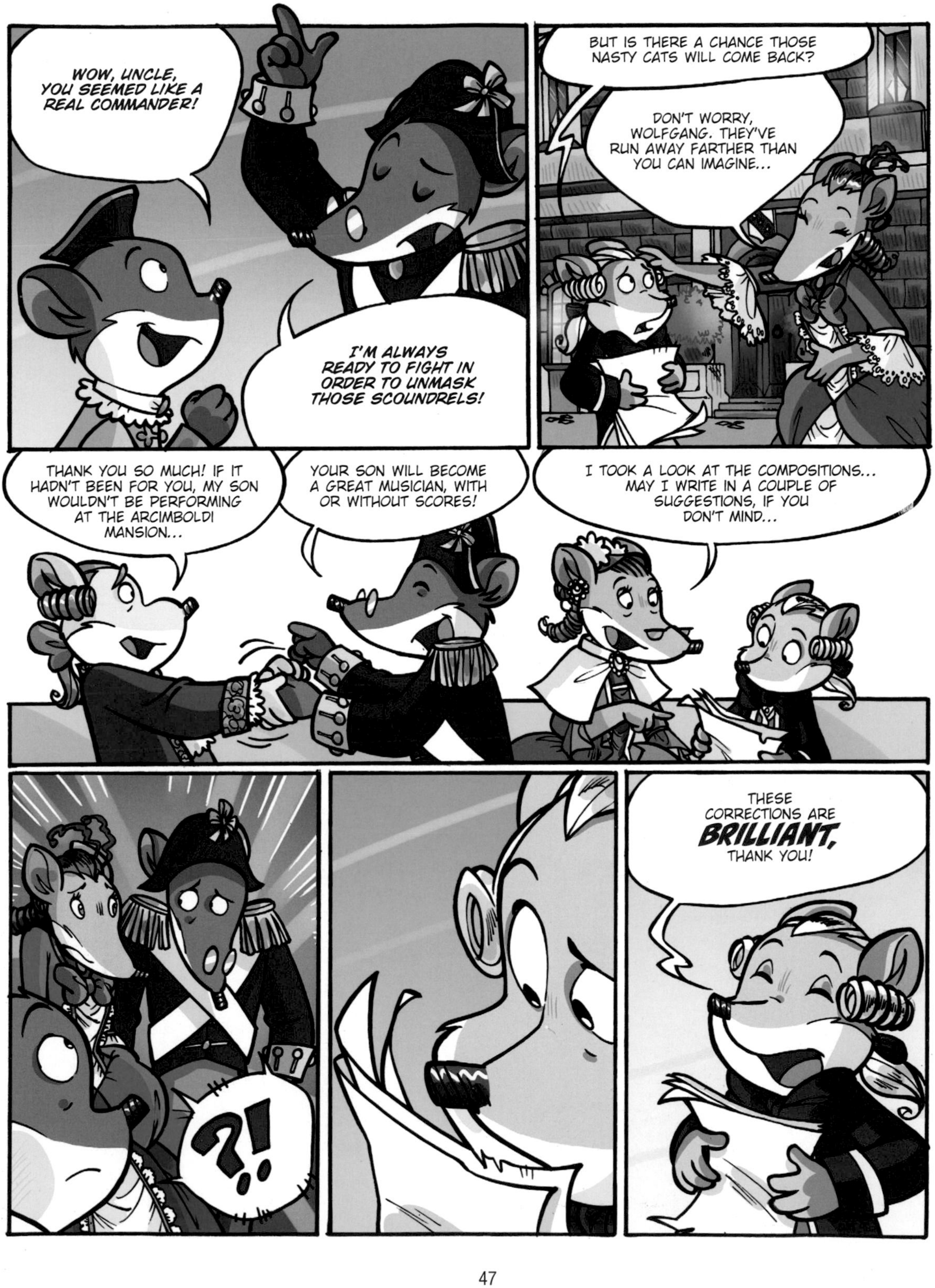

WOW, UNCLE, YOU SEEMED LIKE A REAL COMMANDER!
I'M ALWAYS READY TO FIGHT IN ORDER TO UNMASK THOSE SCOUNDRELS!
BUT IS THERE A CHANCE THOSE NASTY CATS WILL COME BACK?
DON'T WORRY, WOLFGANG. THEY'VE RUN AWAY FARTHER THAN YOU CAN IMAGINE...
THANK YOU SO MUCH! IF IT HADN'T BEEN FOR YOU, MY SON WOULDN'T BE PERFORMING AT THE ARCIMBOLDI MANSION...
YOUR SON WILL BECOME A GREAT MUSICIAN, WITH OR WITHOUT SCORES!
I TOOK A LOOK AT THE COMPOSITIONS... MAY I WRITE IN A COUPLE OF SUGGESTIONS, IF YOU DON'T MIND...
?!
THESE CORRECTIONS ARE BRILLIANT, THANK YOU!

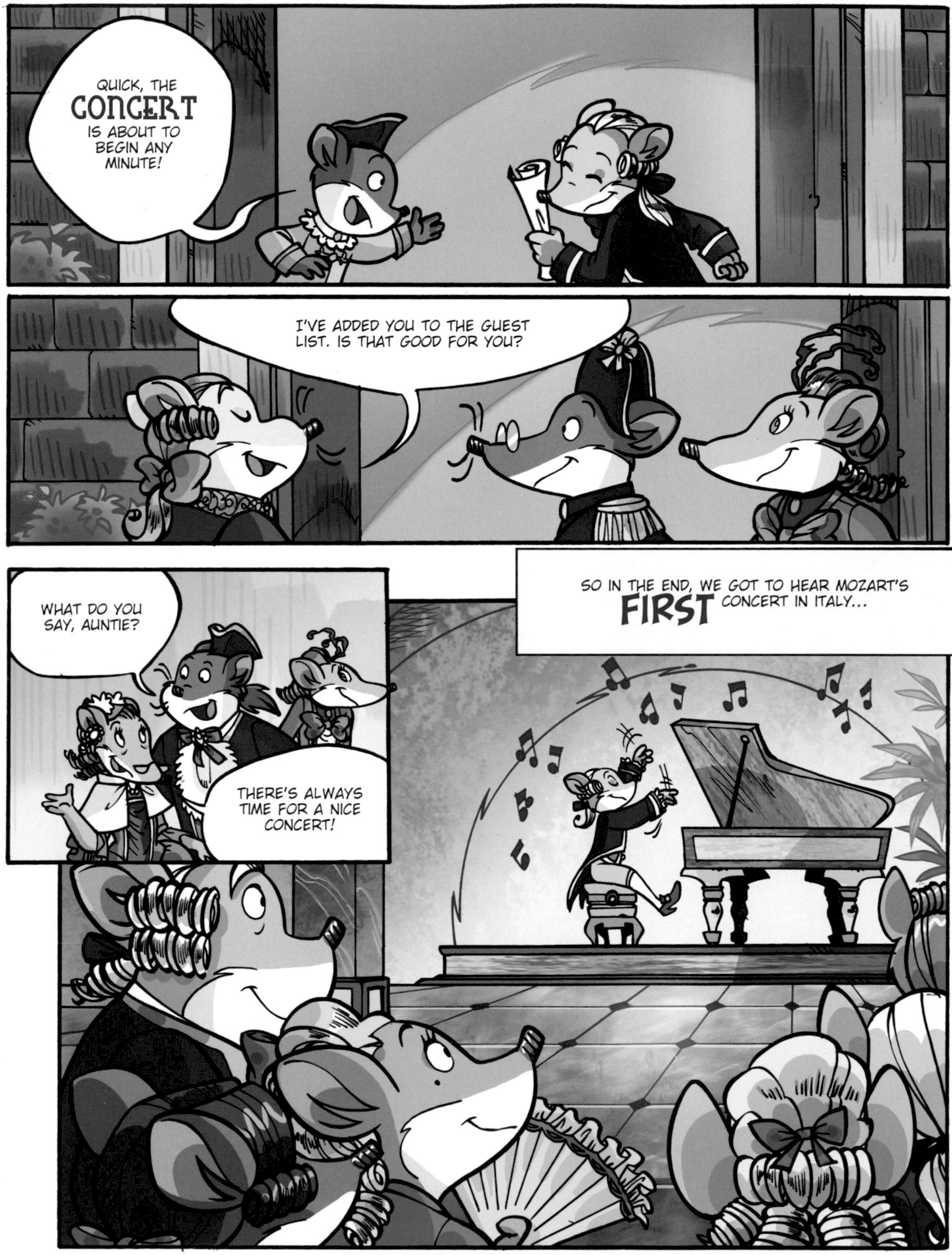
QUICK, THE CONCERT IS ABOUT TO BEGIN ANY MINUTE!
I'VE ADDED YOU TO THE GUEST LIST. IS THAT GOOD FOR YOU?
WHAT DO YOU SAY, AUNTIE?
THERE'S ALWAYS TIME FOR A NICE CONCERT!
SO IN THE END, WE GOT TO HEAR MOZART'S FIRST CONCERT IN ITALY...

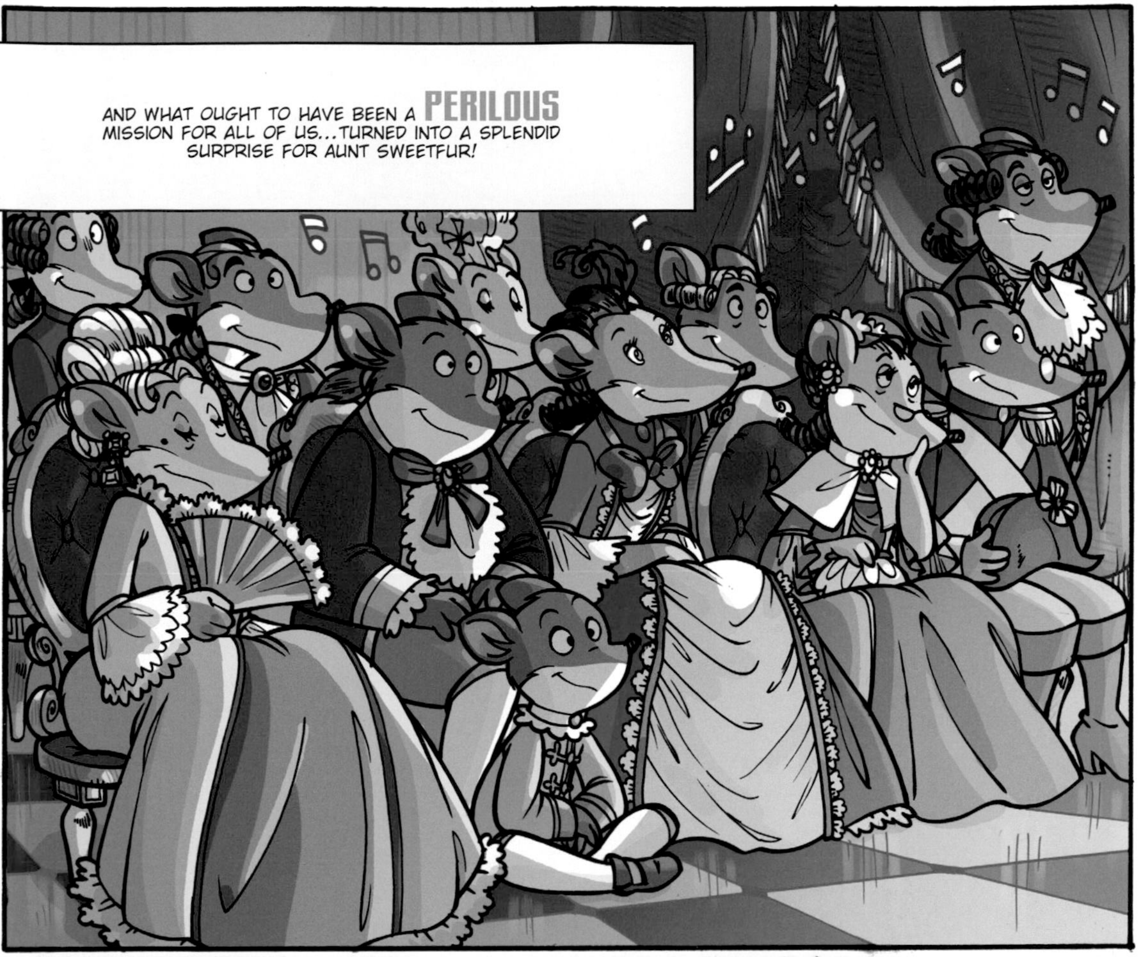
AND WHAT OUGHT TO HAVE BEEN A PERILOUS MISSION FOR ALL OF US...TURNED INTO A SPLENDID SURPRISE FOR AUNT SWEETFUR!

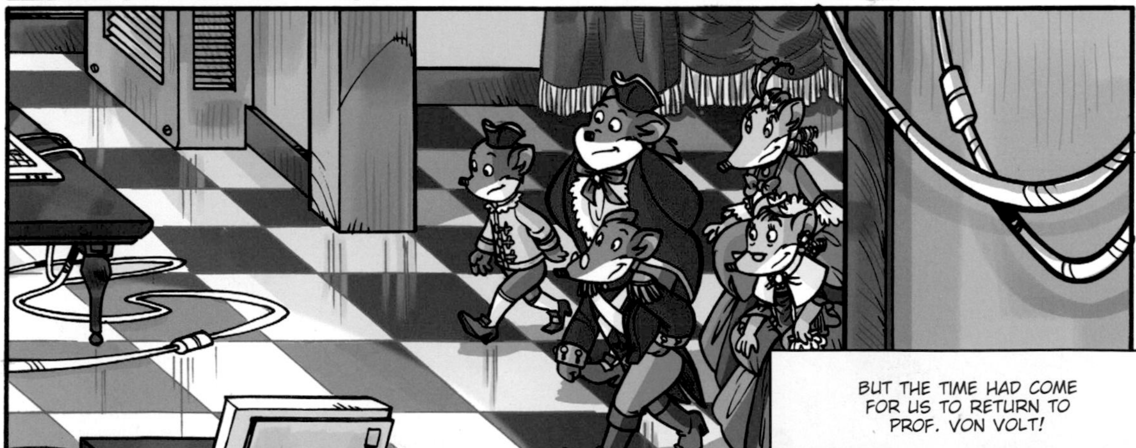
BUT THE TIME HAD COME FOR US TO RETURN TO PROF. VON VOLT!

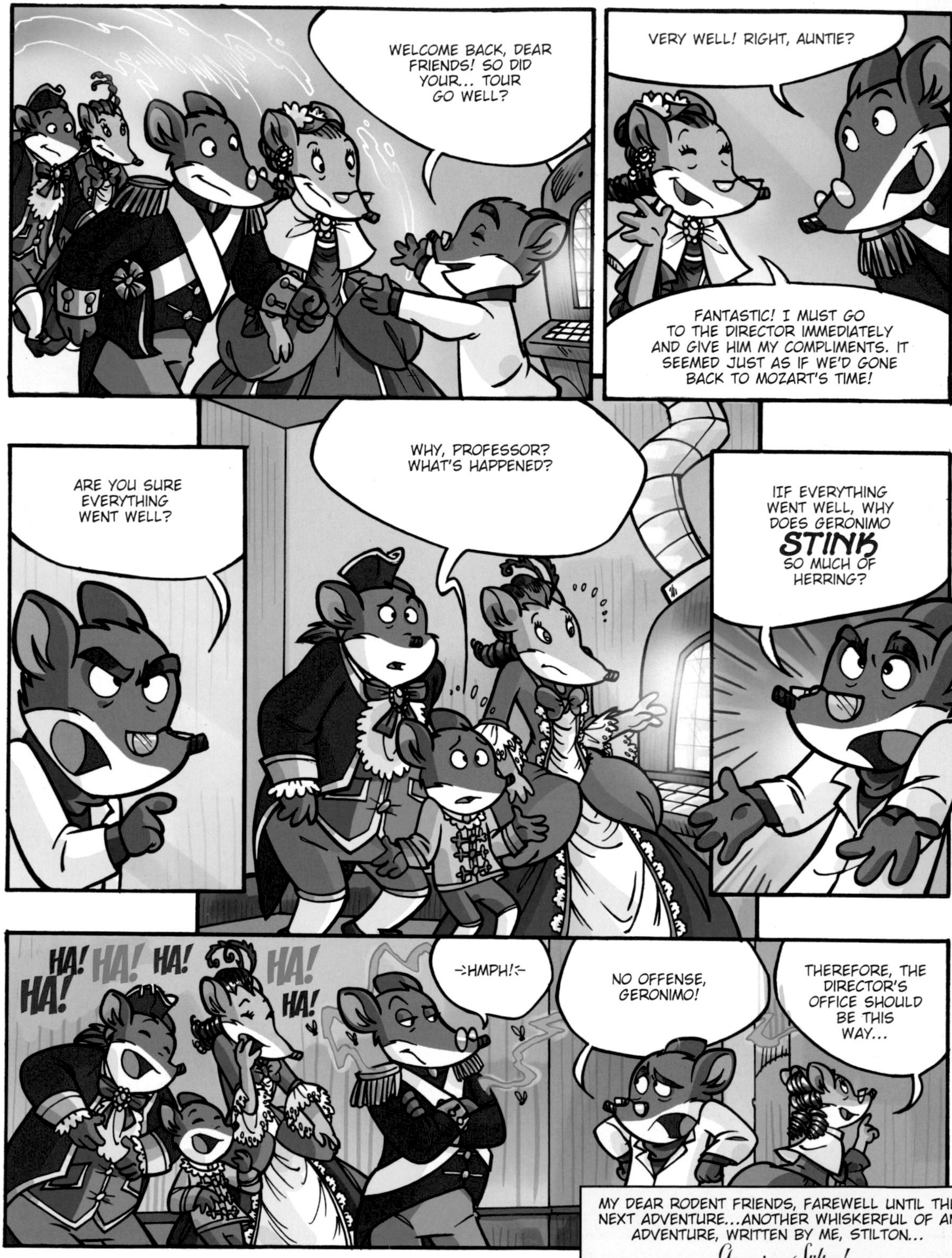
WELCOME BACK, DEAR FRIENDS! SO DID YOUR... TOUR GO WELL?
VERY WELL! RIGHT, AUNTIE?
FANTASTIC! I MUST GO TO THE DIRECTOR IMMEDIATELY AND GIVE HIM MY COMPLIMENTS. IT SEEMED JUST AS IF WE'D GONE BACK TO MOZART'S TIME!
ARE YOU SURE EVERYTHING WENT WELL?
WHY, PROFESSOR? WHAT'S HAPPENED?
IIF EVERYTHING WENT WELL, WHY DOES GERONIMO STINK SO MUCH OF HERRING?
HA! HA! HA! HA! HA! HA!
-HMPH!-
NO OFFENSE, GERONIMO!
THEREFORE, THE DIRECTOR'S OFFICE SHOULD BE THIS WAY...
MY DEAR RODENT FRIENDS, FAREWELL UNTIL THE NEXT ADVENTURE...ANOTHER WHISKERFUL OF AN ADVENTURE, WRITTEN BY ME, STILTON...
Geronimo Stilton!

# Watch Out For PAPERCUTZ™

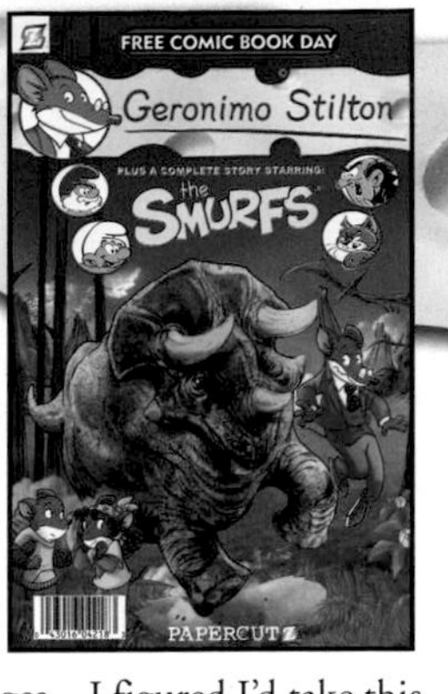
FREE COMIC BOOK DAY
Geronimo Stilton
PLUS A COMPLETE STORY STARRING:
the SMURFS
PAPERCUTZ

Papercutz Editor-in-chief, Jim Salicrup, asked me to write the "Watch Out for Papercutz" page for this very special GERONIMO STILTON graphic novel featuring a magical musical tour of Italy in the 18th Century! While Jim's busy working on such new and exciting Papercutz series such as ERNEST & REBECCA and SYBIL THE BACKPACK FAIRY—check out the mini-previews on the following pages—I figured I'd take this opportunity to tell you all about the big GERONIMO STILTON author tour that took place early May 2011. Oops! I almost forgot--I'm Petranek, *Michael Petranek*, Papercutz Associate Editor.

For several years now, there's been a very special day set aside, usually the first Saturday in May, to celebrate comicbooks. Comicbook stores all over North America celebrate by giving away specially created comicbooks for free! It's called Free Comic Book Day, and this year Papercutz was a Gold-level sponsor of a free comicbook starring GERONIMO STILTON and THE SMURFS. The idea is to not only offer a special treat to regular comicbook fans, but to tempt those that may not already being reading comics or graphic novels to try a few at no risk.

Being that this was the very first free comicbook from Papercutz we wanted to make it as special as possible. This comic presents a lengthy excerpt from GERONIMO STILTON #7 "Dinosaurs in Action," which does a wonderful job of introducing not only Geronimo Stilton, but Benjamin and Bugsy Wugsy, Trap Stilton, Professor Von Volt, and the Pirate Cats to potential new GERONIMO STILTON fans. And as a special treat, especially in light of the new Smurfs movie, we also managed to squeeze in 18 SMURFS comic strips and a complete SMURFS comics story "The Smurf Submarine." But that's not all! As luck would have it, GERONIMO STILTON writers and artists Michele Foschini, Ennio Bufi, and Leonardo Favia were planning to come to the United States to celebrate Children's Book Week. That's right—while Geronimo, Thea, Benjamin, and Aunt Sweetfur visit Italy in this graphic novel, Michele, Ennio, and Leonardo came from Italy to visit the US! The three visited bookstores in the San Francisco Bay Area where they met and greeted GERONIMO STILTON fans, sketched GERONIMO STILTON characters, and talked to kids about making comics.

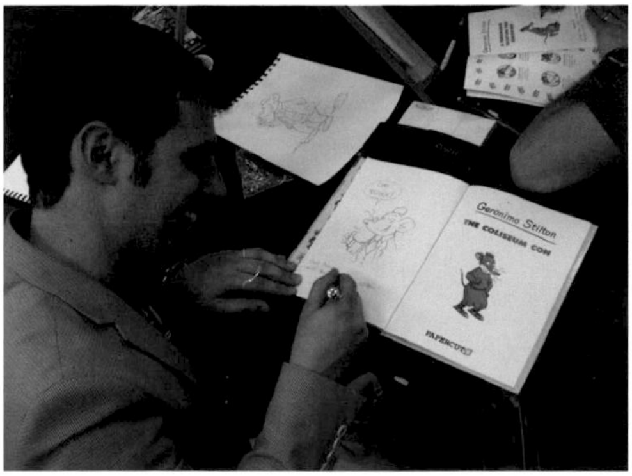
Geronimo Stilton
THE COLISEUM CON
PAPERCUTZ

On Saturday May 7th, Michele, Ennio, and Leonardo all drove down to Atlantis Fantasyworld and Lee's Comics near Santa Cruz, CA to celebrate Free Comic Book Day and the release of GERONIMO STILTON AND THE SMURFS Free comicbook. Crowds of both comicbook fans and GERONIMO STILTON fans were delighted to meet the GS creative crew.

Oh, before I go, I must tell you to check out the new and improved GERONIMO STILTON website! It's more fun, more informative, and more exciting than ever! Be sure to visit www.geronimostilton.com for all the latest GS news, and don't forget to drop by www.papercutz.com to find out what's new at Papercutz. So, until next time, thanks for stopping by, and watch out for Papercutz!

Thanks,
-Michael

# Special Romantic Excerpt from CLASSICS ILLUSTRATED DELUXE #6 "The Three Musketeers"...

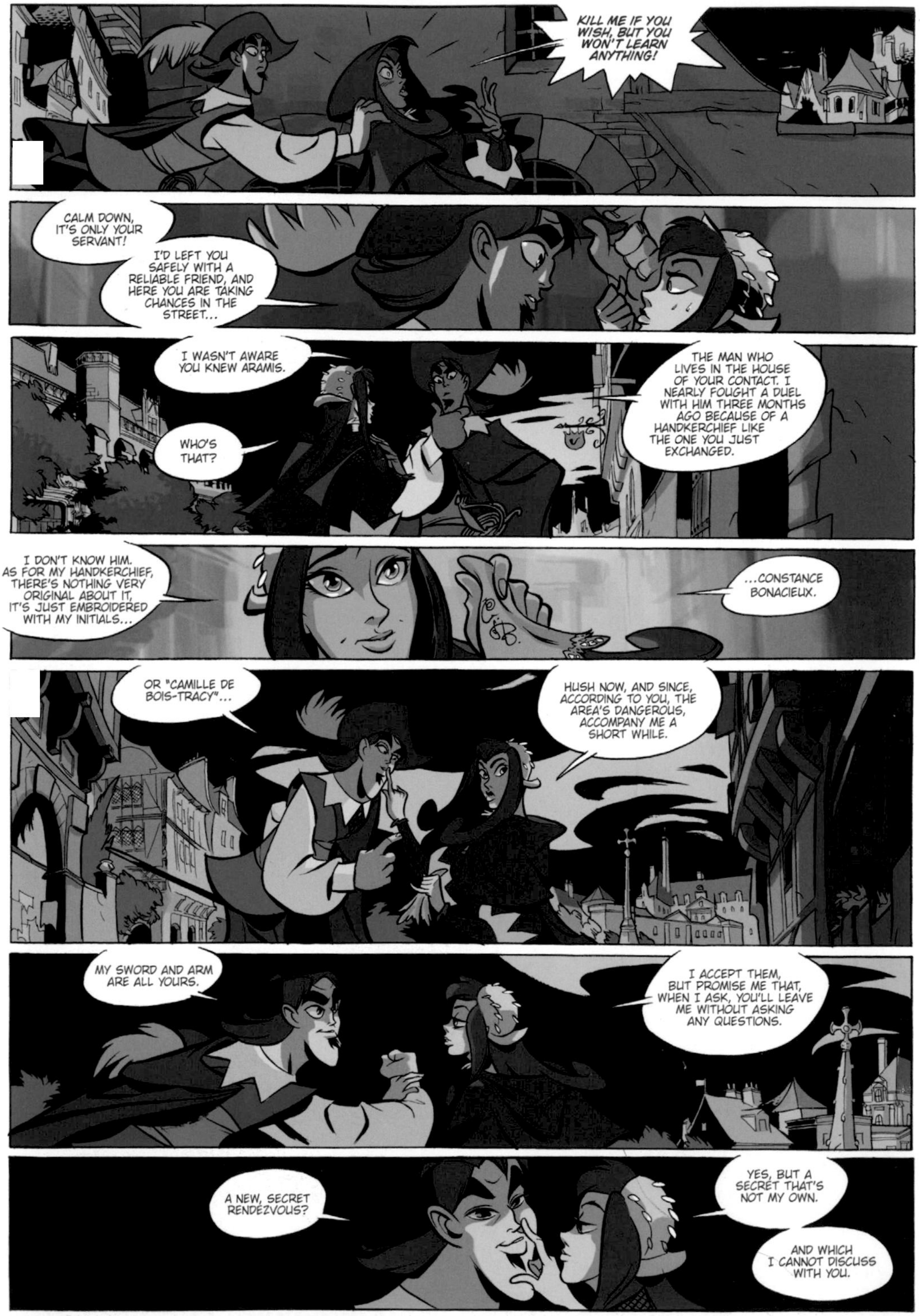
KILL ME IF YOU WISH, BUT YOU WON'T LEARN ANYTHING!
CALM DOWN, IT'S ONLY YOUR SERVANT!
I'D LEFT YOU SAFELY WITH A RELIABLE FRIEND, AND HERE YOU ARE TAKING CHANCES IN THE STREET...
I WASN'T AWARE YOU KNEW ARAMIS.
WHO'S THAT?
THE MAN WHO LIVES IN THE HOUSE OF YOUR CONTACT. I NEARLY FOUGHT A DUEL WITH HIM THREE MONTHS AGO BECAUSE OF A HANDKERCHIEF LIKE THE ONE YOU JUST EXCHANGED.
I DON'T KNOW HIM. AS FOR MY HANDKERCHIEF, THERE'S NOTHING VERY ORIGINAL ABOUT IT, IT'S JUST EMBROIDERED WITH MY INITIALS...
...CONSTANCE BONACIEUX.
OR "CAMILLE DE BOIS-TRACY"...
HUSH NOW, AND SINCE, ACCORDING TO YOU, THE AREA'S DANGEROUS, ACCOMPANY ME A SHORT WHILE.
MY SWORD AND ARM ARE ALL YOURS.
I ACCEPT THEM, BUT PROMISE ME THAT, WHEN I ASK, YOU'LL LEAVE ME WITHOUT ASKING ANY QUESTIONS.
A NEW, SECRET RENDEZVOUS?
YES, BUT A SECRET THAT'S NOT MY OWN.
AND WHICH I CANNOT DISCUSS WITH YOU.

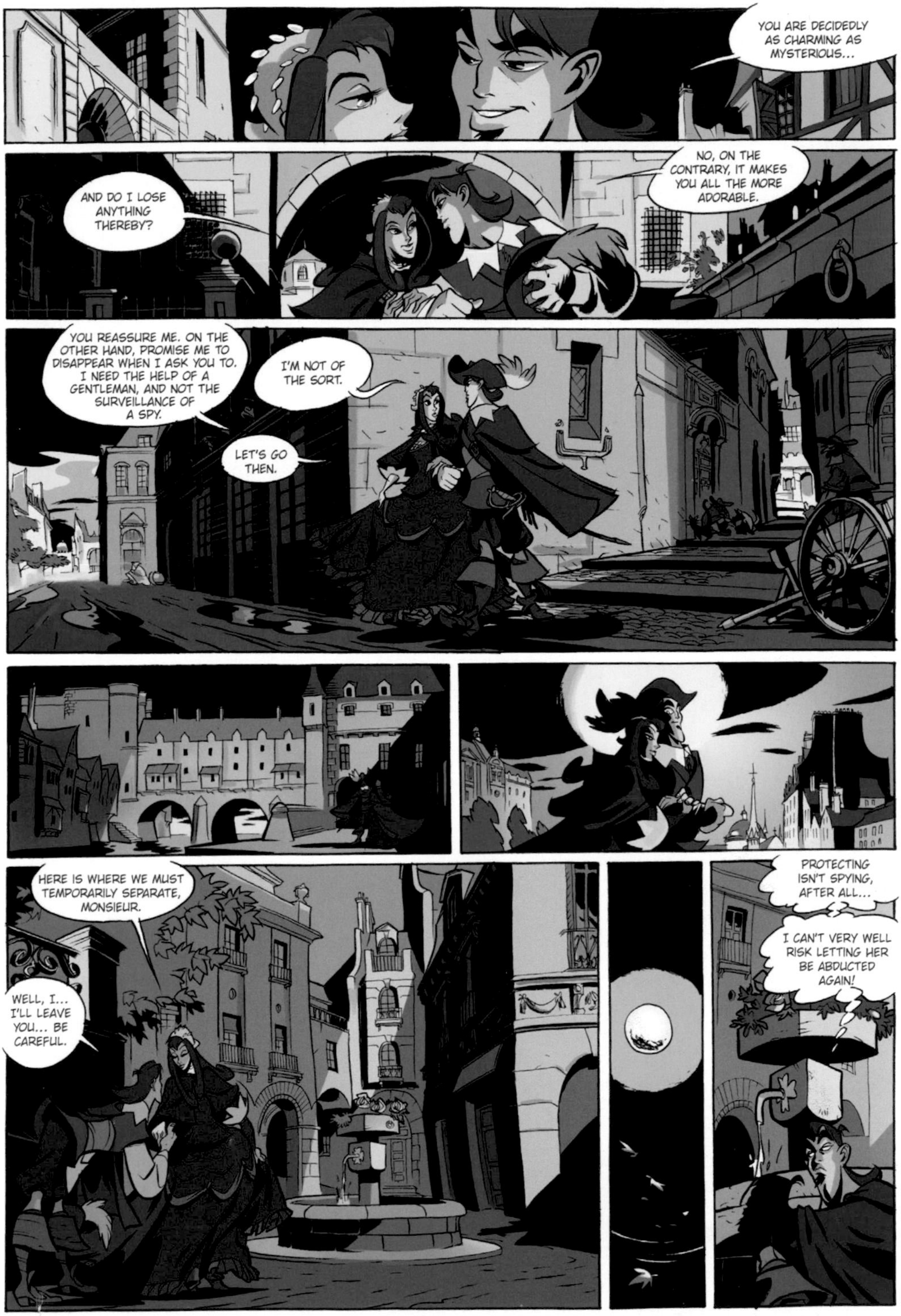
YOU ARE DECIDEDLY AS CHARMING AS MYSTERIOUS...
AND DO I LOSE ANYTHING THEREBY?
NO, ON THE CONTRARY, IT MAKES YOU ALL THE MORE ADORABLE.
YOU REASSURE ME. ON THE OTHER HAND, PROMISE ME TO DISAPPEAR WHEN I ASK YOU TO. I NEED THE HELP OF A GENTLEMAN, AND NOT THE SURVEILLANCE OF A SPY.
I'M NOT OF THE SORT.
LET'S GO THEN.
HERE IS WHERE WE MUST TEMPORARILY SEPARATE, MONSIEUR.
WELL, I... I'LL LEAVE YOU... BE CAREFUL.
PROTECTING ISN'T SPYING, AFTER ALL...
I CAN'T VERY WELL RISK LETTING HER BE ABDUCTED AGAIN!

Special preview of ERNEST & REBECCA #1 "My Best Friend is a Germ"

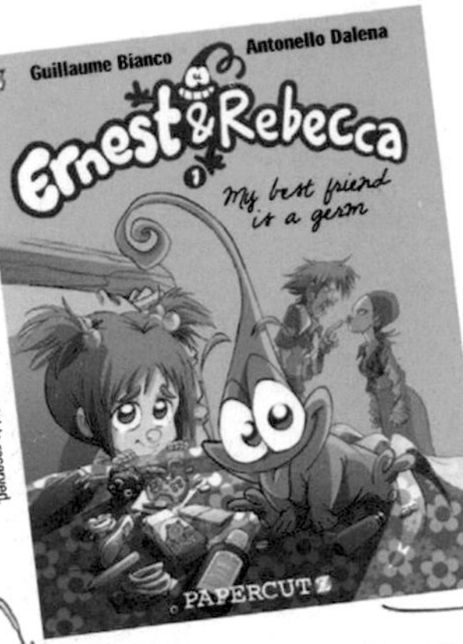
Guillaume Bianco
Antonello Dalena
Ernest & Rebecca
1
My best friend is a germ
PAPERCUTZ



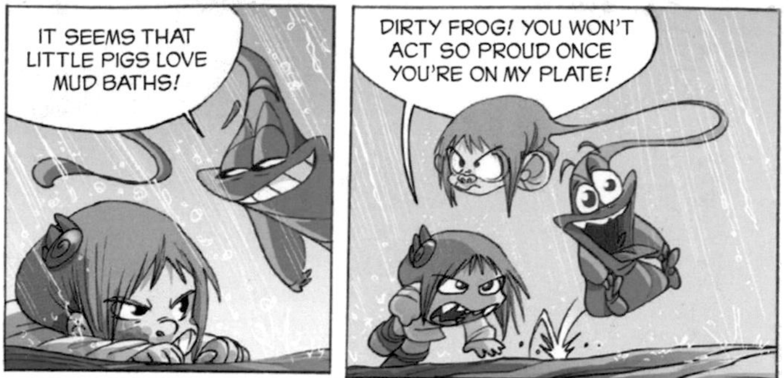
IT SEEMS THAT LITTLE PIGS LOVE MUD BATHS!
DIRTY FROG! YOU WON'T ACT SO PROUD ONCE YOU'RE ON MY PLATE!

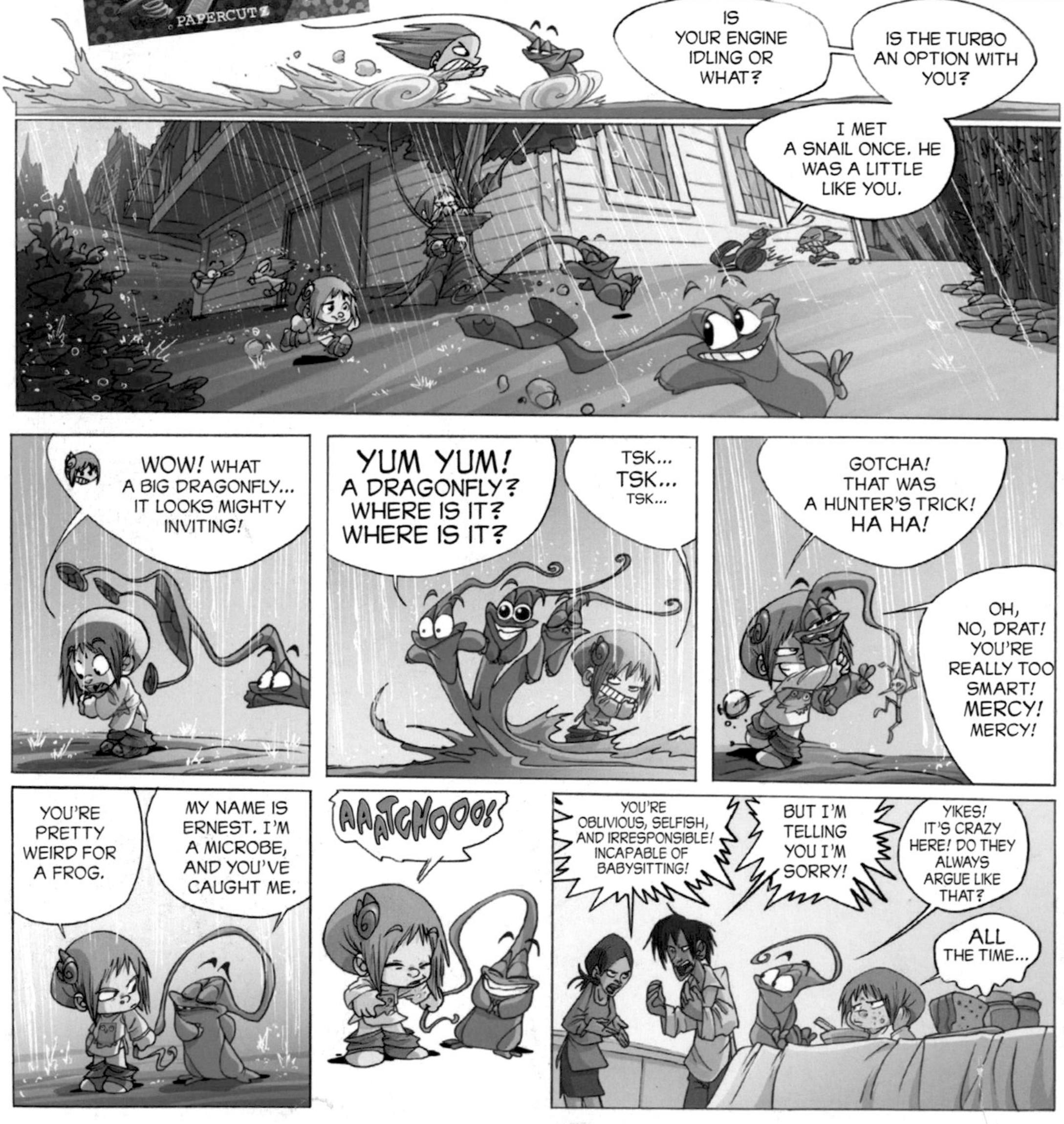
IS YOUR ENGINE IDLING OR WHAT?
IS THE TURBO AN OPTION WITH YOU?
I MET A SNAIL ONCE. HE WAS A LITTLE LIKE YOU.
WOW! WHAT A BIG DRAGONFLY... IT LOOKS MIGHTY INVITING!
YUM YUM! A DRAGONFLY? WHERE IS IT? WHERE IS IT?
TSK... TSK... TSK...
GOTCHA! THAT WAS A HUNTER'S TRICK! HA HA!
OH, NO, DRAT! YOU'RE REALLY TOO SMART! MERCY! MERCY!
YOU'RE PRETTY WEIRD FOR A FROG.
MY NAME IS ERNEST. I'M A MICROBE, AND YOU'VE CAUGHT ME.
AAATCHOOO!
YOU'RE OBLIVIOUS, SELFISH, AND IRRESPONSIBLE! INCAPABLE OF BABYSITTING!
BUT I'M TELLING YOU I'M SORRY!
YIKES! IT'S CRAZY HERE! DO THEY ALWAYS ARGUE LIKE THAT?
ALL THE TIME...

Don't miss ERNEST & REBECCA #1 "My Best Friend is a Germ"

Special preview of

SYBIL THE BACKPACK FAIRY #1 "Nina"

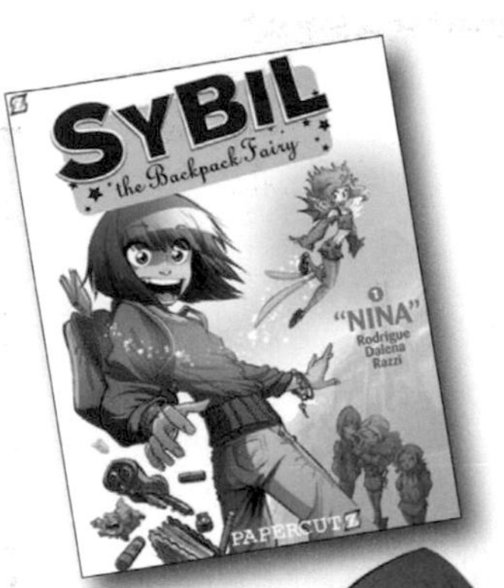
SYBIL
the Backpack Fairy
1
"NINA"
Rodrigue
Dalena
Razzi
PAPERCUTZ

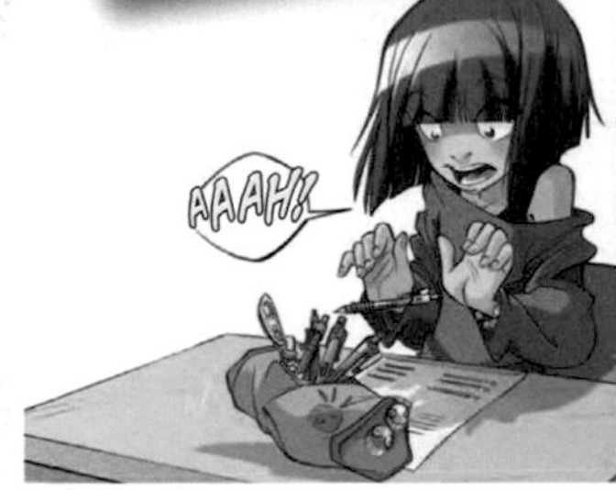
AAAH!

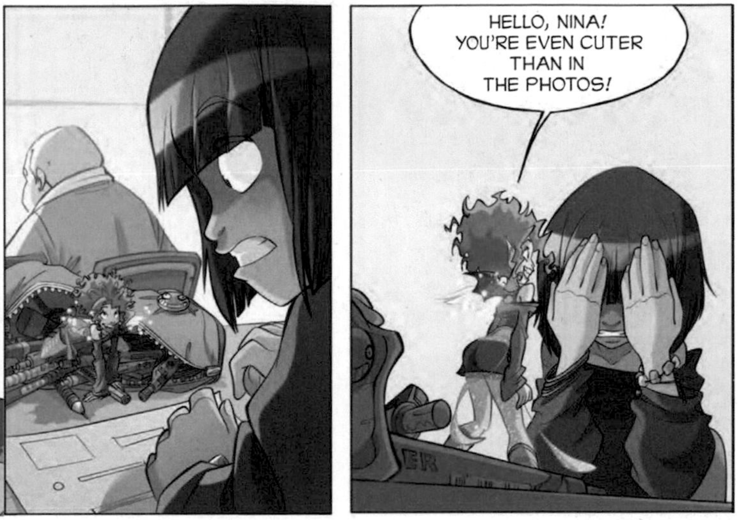
HELLO, NINA! YOU'RE EVEN CUTER THAN IN THE PHOTOS!



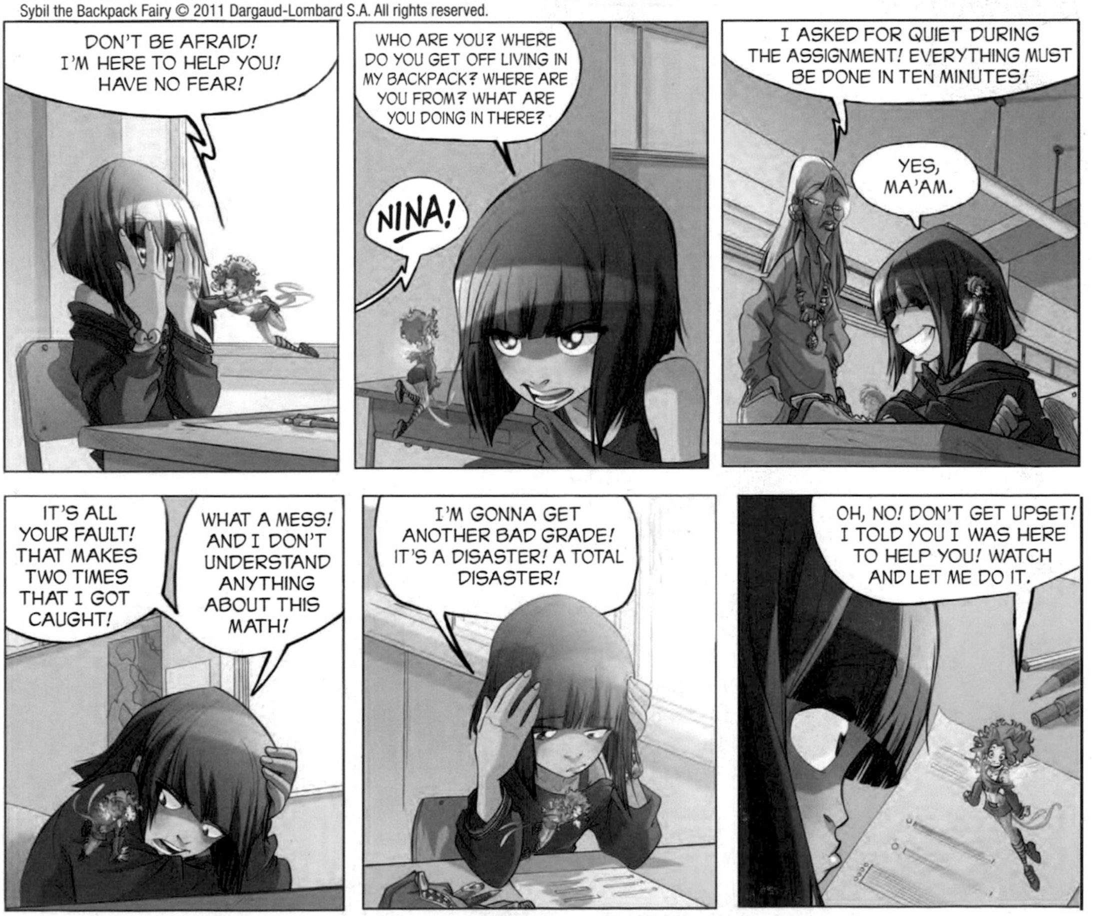
DON'T BE AFRAID! I'M HERE TO HELP YOU! HAVE NO FEAR!
WHO ARE YOU? WHERE DO YOU GET OFF LIVING IN MY BACKPACK? WHERE ARE YOU FROM? WHAT ARE YOU DOING IN THERE?
NINA!
I ASKED FOR QUIET DURING THE ASSIGNMENT! EVERYTHING MUST BE DONE IN TEN MINUTES!
YES, MA'AM.
IT'S ALL YOUR FAULT! THAT MAKES TWO TIMES THAT I GOT CAUGHT!
WHAT A MESS! AND I DON'T UNDERSTAND ANYTHING ABOUT THIS MATH!
I'M GONNA GET ANOTHER BAD GRADE! IT'S A DISASTER! A TOTAL DISASTER!
OH, NO! DON'T GET UPSET! I TOLD YOU I WAS HERE TO HELP YOU! WATCH AND LET ME DO IT.

Don't miss SYBIL THE BACKPACK FAIRY #1 "Nina"

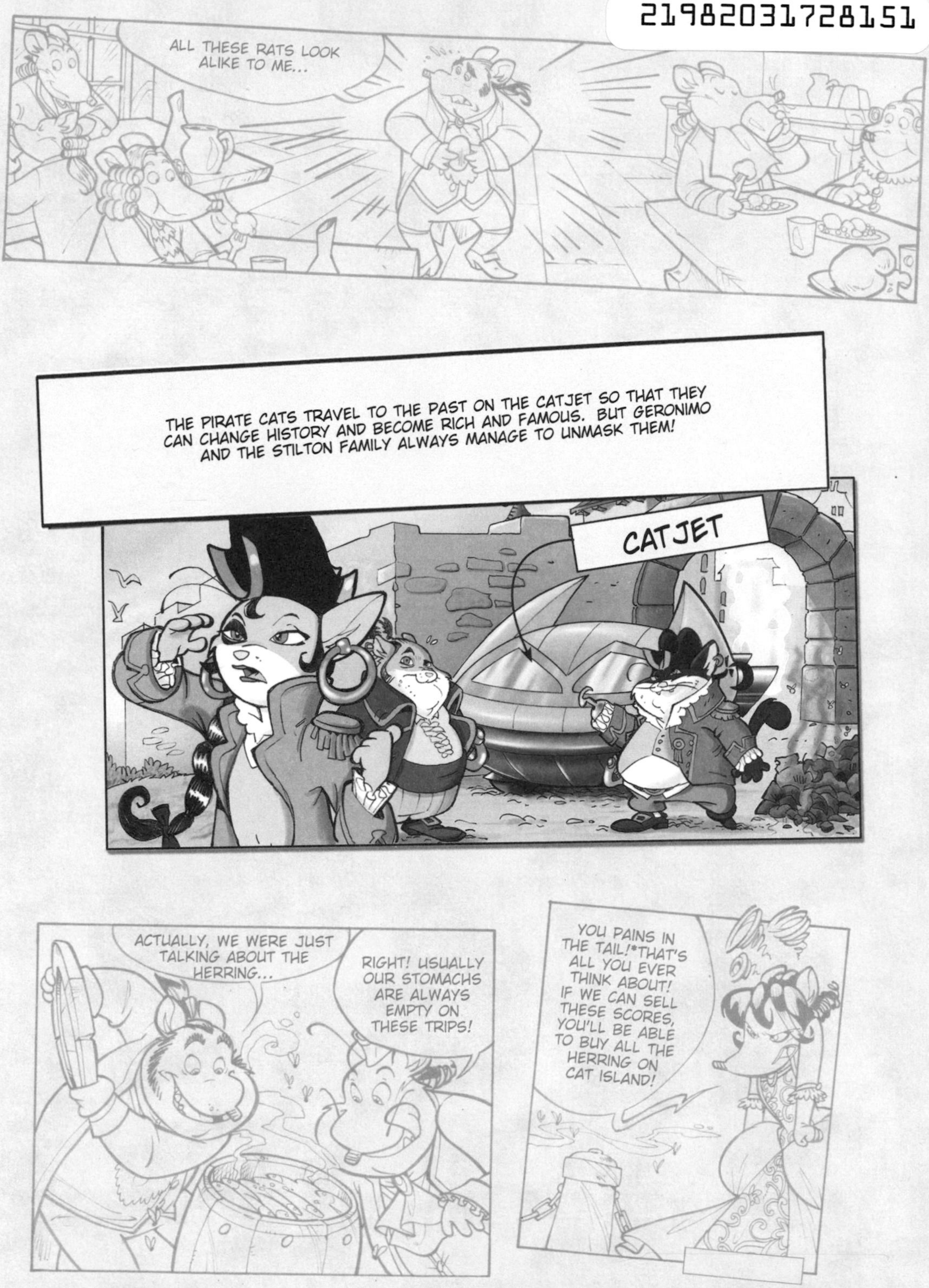
ALL THESE RATS LOOK ALIKE TO ME...
THE PIRATE CATS TRAVEL TO THE PAST ON THE CATJET SO THAT THEY CAN CHANGE HISTORY AND BECOME RICH AND FAMOUS. BUT GERONIMO AND THE STILTON FAMILY ALWAYS MANAGE TO UNMASK THEM!
CATJET
ACTUALLY, WE WERE JUST TALKING ABOUT THE HERRING...
RIGHT! USUALLY OUR STOMACHS ARE ALWAYS EMPTY ON THESE TRIPS!
YOU PAINS IN THE TAIL!*THAT'S ALL YOU EVER THINK ABOUT! IF WE CAN SELL THESE SCORES, YOU'LL BE ABLE TO BUY ALL THE HERRING ON CAT ISLAND!